Shahana

TITLES IN THIS SERIES

THROUGH MY EYES
series editor Lyn White

Shahana

ROSANNE HAWKE

ALLEN&UNWIN
SYDNEY • MELBOURNE • AUCKLAND • LONDON

Australian Government

This project has been assisted by the Australian Government through
the Australia Council, its arts funding and advisory body.

*A portion of the proceeds (up to $5000) from sales of this series will be donated to UNICEF.
UNICEF works in over 190 countries, including those in which books in this series are
set, to promote and protect the rights of children.   www.unicef.org.au*

First published in 2013
Copyright © Text, Rosanne Hawke 2013
Copyright © Series concept and series creator, Lyn White 2013

Allen & Unwin
83 Alexander Street, Crows Nest NSW 2065, Australia
Phone: (61 2) 8425 0100
Email: info@allenandunwin.com
Web: www.allenandunwin.com

A Cataloguing-in-Publication entry is available from
the National Library of Australia – www.trove.nla.gov.au

ISBN 978 1 74331 246 9

Teachers notes available from www.allenandunwin.com

Cover and text design by Bruno Herfst & Vincent Agostino
Cover photos by Getty Images/mark25 (girl); Yasir Nisar (valley)
Set in 10.5pt Plantin
This book was printed in February 2015 at Griffin Press,
168 Cross Keys Road, Salisbury South, South Australia 5106, Australia

10 9 8 7

For the children of conflict;
may you dream without fear.

—o—o—o—

If Paradise exists on the planet Earth
It is here, it is here, it is here.

Nur ad-Din Abd ar-Rahman Jami,
as quoted by Emperor Jahangir
upon seeing Kashmir

True peace is not merely the absence
of tension: it is the presence of justice.

It is love that will save our world and
our civilisation, love even for enemies.

Martin Luther King Jr

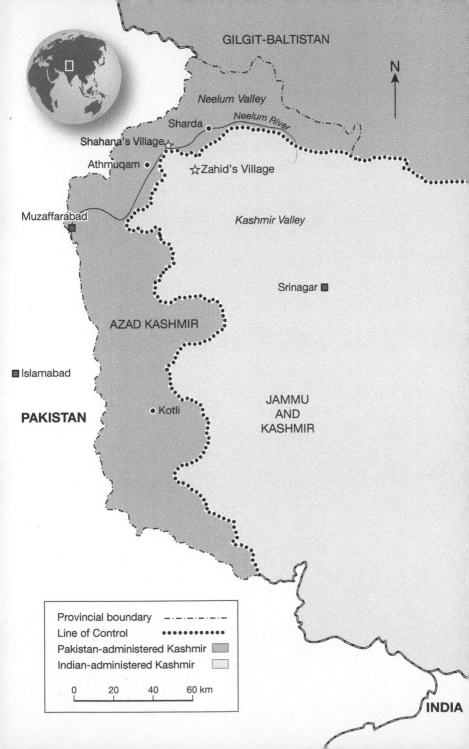

Chapter 1

The early sun was shining as Shahana skipped down the village bazaar. Her beloved big brother Irfan was taking her to the tent school. Their cement school had never been rebuilt after the earthquake. Shahana had on her blue qameez and white shalwar; she was nine and had just learned how to iron her school uniform. Today would be exciting: she had two new apples in her backpack, one for herself and one for Ayesha, her friend from the next class.

'Assalamu alaikum, peace be upon you,' called Mr Pervaiz from his shop with the new glass windows. 'Wa alaikum assalam, and upon you be peace,' Irfan responded. They stopped by the door and Mr Pervaiz gave them each a toffee. He pinched Shahana on the cheek. 'What an angel,' he said.

Just as Irfan drew her away towards the road there was a thump from an RPG; then the shelling started. Mr Pervaiz's new windows burst like a bubble. Glass sprayed

over the road and Irfan pushed Shahana to the ground,
dropping to cover her.

Shahana wakes up gasping. She hasn't dreamed this dream for a long time. *Dreams are never true*, she reminds herself, but she can't stop the memory, can't stop her heart racing, as if a black leopard is chasing her. It wasn't just Irfan: her mother was there too, and her little brother, Tanveer, who has hated loud noises ever since that day. Ever since, his breathing has been worse, as though something sharp stuck in his chest. The banging of the guns went on forever. She could see Tanveer screaming in her mother's arms, even though she couldn't hear him. And when the gunfire stopped, Irfan didn't get up. Nor did her mother.

It was her father who found Shahana and Tanveer. He wept as he took them to Nana-ji, her mother's father, who lived in the forest. Their own wooden house in the village had burned with the gunfire. Shahana never went back to school after that. Instead, she did all her mother's jobs and looked after Tanveer. She wishes she could study again but there is no school in the village now, and besides, she can't make money at school.

Shahana can still hear the gunfire. Is it following her waking hours now, too? Her heart is still beating wildly; she will feel dizzy next. She takes a deep breath to slow the thumping.

Tanveer wakes with a cry. They sleep in the same charpoy, a string bed, and she puts an arm around him. 'Chup, quiet, it will stop soon.' She hopes it will, for she realises now that the gunfire is real. It is coming from down near the big Neelum River, where the Line of Control runs along the border between Azad Kashmir and Jammu and Kashmir. A dog howls.

'See,' she says, 'the soldiers are just frightening the dogs away.' But Shahana isn't so sure. There is supposed to be a ceasefire on the Line of Control. Indian soldiers patrol the electric fence to stop militants infiltrating their side of Kashmir, and Pakistani soldiers patrol it to keep an eye on the Indian soldiers, but both sides take shots at each other across the high razor wire. Pity anyone who gets in the way.

She takes more slow breaths to steady herself and shuts her mind against the thought. It is too much for one night. Tanveer takes shallow little breaths. When he cries he finds it hard to breathe.

'Tomorrow we will go to the village.' Shahana strokes the hair away from Tanveer's temples and feels his breathing ease. She covers him with the cotton-filled quilt and lies down, facing him, even though she can't see him. In his hand she can feel the tiny carved camel Nana-ji made for him. It has a separate calf inside, yet Nana-ji carved it out of one piece of wood. It rattles as Tanveer moves his arm under the quilt.

Tanveer is only nine and looks younger. He can't milk the goat yet, but at least he can collect wood in the forest for their cooking fire. Even then, she has to fight an urge to go with him. He tends to wander and forget where he is; what if he gets lost or falls in the river? He is the only family she has left. She knows she loves him but

3

it is so difficult to feel it, to feel like a mother. Sometimes Shahana feels like the legendary stone princess, who was so beautiful that two princes both wanted to marry her. She prayed that they would all be turned to stone, so the princes wouldn't kill each other. When Shahana's heart isn't pounding, it is cold like stone.

Chapter 2

Shahana hurries to pack the embroidery she has done for Mr Nadir at the cloth shop. If she is late she might not get paid for her work, and she needs the money to buy vegetables, and medicine for Tanveer.

'Shahji?'

Shahana smiles. It is what Tanveer has called her since he was little.

He pokes his head around their carved door. 'Are we going to the village yet?'

'Ji hahn, yes.' She puts the last dupatta, a long silk scarf, into her backpack and stands up. 'Rope up Rani, Tanveer.' She watches him from the doorway as he ties the goat under the house. Rani shakes her head and bleats in time to her bell.

'A jao, come, let's go.' Shahana walks down the log ramp as Tanveer skips up to her. They pass their grand-father's roses, and the spring where they wash their plates and pots. The water slaps onto the rocks and white froth flies up.

Tanveer runs ahead and swivels to look at her. 'You're slow, Shahji.' It is not raining today, although the grass is wet and slippery; soon there will be slush from snow to walk through. She is about to warn him to be careful when his face changes. The grin disappears. 'Look.' He points up the mountain behind them. 'There's a big dog.'

'It's probably wild. Ignore it, Tanveer.'

He keeps twisting to see the dog as they make their way down the forest path on the mountain slope. 'Stop worrying about it, Tanveer. We must hurry.'

'You don't like them either.' It sounds like an accusation. She takes his hand until they come to the log bridge over the stream. Here they have to walk in single file.

The bridge is made up of two logs reaching from one bank to a rock in the middle of the stream and another two logs joining the rock to the other side. Planks of wood are nailed across the logs. Every time they put their feet down, the planks groan and shudder. Glancing down, Shahana can see the white water clawing up to the bridge. The roar of the water is almost as loud as the Neelum River. She hesitates, but Tanveer pulls her forward. Shahana tries to think logically. Grown men heavier than her use this bridge every day and it holds them. She gives Tanveer a smile as he looks back at her; no need to show him her fear.

They reach the dirt road that leads to the village. They don't come this way often, so there are many things to capture Tanveer's attention. They pass almond trees, and fences made of logs. A man smacks his horse with a piece of leather to make it move. It carries two heavy baskets of wood across its back, although it doesn't look much stronger than Rani. Some children are sitting by the roadside selling apples. If there is money left Shahana will buy one for Tanveer on the way home. They pass houses pockmarked from shelling and gunfire, and smelly gutters, where Tanveer screws up his nose. Finally, they stand outside Mr Nadir's shop. It is the only shop in the village that doesn't show signs of the fighting, for he has enough money to fix it. If Irfan were alive he would bring the embroidery and Shahana wouldn't have to do business with a man like Mr Nadir.

It is early, so there are no customers inside. The counter has a computer on it, and stacked around the walls are many carpets and namdah rugs made from felt. Shahana puts the backpack on the counter in front of Mr Nadir. He moves some papier-mâché boxes and carved wooden plates out of the way. Shahana's gaze follows the boxes. She has one, in the shape of a heart. It was her mother's. Her father found it after the fighting. She chases the thought away with a little shake of her head, and her round silver earrings jingle. They, too, were her mother's.

Mr Nadir doesn't say anything at first. He puts his cigarette between his last two fingers and carefully lifts out a dupatta. He checks the tiny stitches around the border, then he takes out the red pashmina shawl, the side panels embroidered with orange thread. Shahana has tried especially hard with the chinar tree pattern.

The shawl looks like the forest when the leaves change colour. Mr Nadir grunts.

Shahana holds Tanveer's hand so he remembers to stay silent. She watches Mr Nadir's face. It is difficult to tell whether he is pleased or disappointed.

He takes out the other dupattas. 'Accha,' he finally says, 'it is good enough.' His praise is grudging but Shahana lets out a breath.

Mr Nadir stares at her. 'You are Zafir's grand-daughter in talent, it seems. More skilful than your father at least.' His tone darkens as he speaks of her father. He has never said anything like this to her before and she doesn't know how to reply. Nor does she like the look in his eyes. She stares at the counter to avoid them.

He reaches under the counter and brings out a grey woollen robe. 'Soon I will need to sell embroidered pherans for the winter. You can try this one in green thread. If you do a good job I will give you silver thread to use.' He takes a skein from the glass case under the counter. 'Just embroider here and here.'

Shahana tries not to show how pleased she is to hear of the silver thread. Nana-ji had taught her how to embroider a pheran. Some of the shawls and pherans that Mr Nadir had given Nana-ji to do were stitched by her, especially when his eyes failed before he died last winter. Mr Nadir had never guessed.

Mr Nadir measures the green thread out carefully. 'Do not lose any.' The sharpness in his tone makes her tighten her grip on Tanveer's hand. 'Or it will come out of your pay.'

8

His gaze lingers on Tanveer. 'Does he have your family talent too? His fingers are just the right size for making carpets. He can work for me.' Mr Nadir tilts his head to the door behind him. Shahana looks up at him in horror. Mr Nadir uses the boys who are sold to him to work on his carpet loom. They also weave the shawls that Shahana embroiders. Their families can't find the money to buy the boys back. She could never think of selling Tanveer to Mr Nadir.

She shakes her head and tries to speak calmly. 'Nay, janab, he helps me look after the goat, and collects firewood. I cannot spare him.'

Mr Nadir sneers at her. 'You will bring him one day. You cannot survive here in Azad Kashmir by yourselves.' His voice takes on a speculative tone. 'How old are you now?'

Shahana doesn't answer but asks for her payment instead. Mr Nadir counts out the rupees. It isn't as much as Nana-ji received for the same amount of work but it will be enough for their food. She puts the pheran and thread into her backpack and steers Tanveer out of the shop. She won't bring him next time.

'I could sew as well as you and Nana-ji,' Tanveer says.

Shahana smiles at him. 'I'm sure you will. You just have to keep practising.' Already he has a flair for colour, and she has taught him the simple stitches Nana-ji started her on.

Tanveer skips ahead. There aren't many proper shops left in the tiny bazaar. Like the school, many haven't been rebuilt since the earthquake, and that was years ago. Shahana was only seven then. After that came more fighting; always there has been fighting. There was so much on the day she was born, the forest caught fire.

Tanveer stops outside the teashop. Some men are inside, drinking chai. The teashop is one of the few places in the village with a satellite dish, and the TV is showing the morning news. 'Let's watch,' Tanveer says.

Shahana hesitates, as she always does. It is a man's place and she can't go inside. Her mother once told her that before Kashmir was divided between Pakistan and India, women and men worked and prayed together, but it is different now. Shahana decides it won't hurt to watch from the window; Tanveer has little to fill his mind. Other times they have seen Angrezi, English cartoons, cricket matches or programs on how to pray.

A pretty lady with a shawl over her hair, just like Shahana's, is speaking. 'This morning in Srinagar men are throwing stones,' the lady says. A boy not much older than Shahana appears on the screen. 'We don't want conflict. We want azadi, freedom from the Indian forces and foreign militants. We want to govern ourselves. I throw stones not to hurt but to tell the army and militants to leave Kashmir.'

The footage shows men and boys throwing stones at soldiers in the streets. There is much shouting, and the soldiers fire their weapons.

'I could throw stones a long way too,' Tanveer says. He has never been allowed to throw stones and Shahana pulls him away. A jeep full of Pakistani tourists roars down the bazaar, taking them to one of the bigger villages. They may be the last visitors before the weather closes the valley.

'Come, we must buy our food.' Shahana guides Tanveer past the chickens in cages and goat meat hanging on hooks. All the best cuts of meat will have been bought by now, but she doesn't even check. Her embroidery money is not enough for meat. At Eid when her parents were both alive they had lamb or goat chops cooked in milk, saffron and herbs. Her mother decorated them with pure silver leaf.

They pass the clay pots and stop at Mr Pervaiz's shop, a stall he sets up outside his house.

'Assalamu alaikum, Shahana, Tanveer.' Mr Pervaiz nods at them.

'Wa alaikum assalam,' Shahana gives the required response. Mr Pervaiz has sold vegetables to her family since long before she was born. 'Some of your best onions, potatoes and beans, janab,' she says in the same way her mother used to. Nana-ji said if you have rice and greens, you have everything you need. He said that's what their family had eaten for generations, even though he always bought meat for Shahana and Tanveer to eat.

When Mr Pervaiz tells her the amount, she argues. 'But that is twice the usual price. You know I have little money.' How dare he try to force more from her! If only Nana-ji were here.

Mr Pervaiz spreads his hands. 'I am truly sorry but there has been fighting on the road near the LoC.' He spells out the Angrezi letters that everyone uses to

11

refer to the Line of Control. 'Trucks cannot easily get through, and the one that did charged me danger money. I have to recoup it.'

Shahana knows it is Mr Pervaiz's son-in-law who brings him goods to sell, but Mr Pervaiz truly looks sorry. She sighs and buys fewer onions than usual. Perhaps they can survive with one onion in their curry. Fortunately, she still has aniseed, cardamom and cinnamon. She has some cumin left too – that is the flavour she thinks is tastiest. She buys the tiniest bit of saffron to colour the rice yellow. Tanveer likes that. Mr Pervaiz hands her the saffron in a twist of paper.

'And some rice, please,' Shahana says. Mr Pervaiz pours a jugful from the big hessian sack into a paper bag and weighs it.

'Seven rupees, fifty paisa,' Mr Pervaiz says.

Shahana counts the money out. She lets Tanveer help. He has to learn how to count or he will be cheated in the bazaar. Mr Pervaiz throws a bunch of coriander into her backpack. At least coriander is so cheap it can be given away. She smiles politely at Mr Pervaiz as they leave. He has a concerned look on his face, as though he wants to ask her how she is, but he just lifts his hand in farewell.

She stops at a stall selling second-hand clothes, for she has seen a woollen cap. It has ears like a leopard and costs one rupee. 'Here,' she says to Tanveer. 'This will keep your head warm, since winter is coming. Now you will look like a chitta.' He puts it on quietly and she sighs. It is so hard to make him laugh. The children selling apples are still sitting by the road. Shahana takes out a rupee. The children look as if they need it. A boy not much older than Tanveer hands her two apples. 'Shukriya, thank you,' she says. Behind the children she can see a mound of rubbish with grass growing over it. She pulls Tanveer away before he notices. The mound is where their family home used to be.

At the edge of the village they pass her friend Ayesha's house with its shiny tin roof and small satellite dish, slanted like a hat. Shahana wishes she could talk to Ayesha, but ever since Ayesha's father disappeared, her mother has been called a half-widow, and hasn't opened the door to Shahana. She is too sad and ashamed.

Chapter 3

Shahana wakes to the faint sound of the azan, the call to prayer from the little village mosque. Being careful not to disturb Tanveer, she prays, then takes the plastic bucket outside to milk the goat.

'Rani, what would we do without you?' Shahana rests her forehead on Rani's flank for a moment but she doesn't relax her fingers. Given the chance, Rani would kick that bucket and the milk would be lost. It is the best milk for Tanveer. When he was younger she gave him buffalo milk but it made him so sick he couldn't breathe. She had thought he would die. It was Aunty Rabia who had suggested the goat, back when she wasn't a half-widow.

Rani bleats as Tanveer comes outside to relieve himself. He crouches on the ground away from Shahana, then stands to tie the cord of his shalwar. He seems to have forgotten the noises in the night and pets Rani as she nibbles his qameez.

Shahana finishes the milking. 'We'll have some roti and chai.'

He smiles. 'And then we'll go to the little river?'

'Ji, yes.' He loves the little river, which is just a tributary, but Shahana never feels safe there. It is close to the fast-flowing Neelum River and the Line of Control, with Pakistani and Indian soldiers each patrolling their side of the fence. Besides, there are too many memories.

'Let's go close to the big river. It's where the best fish are. Maybe we'll even see a chitta,' Tanveer says.

'It's too early for chittas and besides, we won't be there long. As soon as we catch a fish we'll come home.' Her words are a warning and Tanveer's smile fades. Shahana feels mean but she has to teach him to be careful.

After their bread and chai, Tanveer takes a cloth bag from the hook behind the door and gives it to Shahana. Nana-ji's rifle is behind the door too, but Shahana has forbidden him to touch it. He races down under the house and slings Nana-ji's fishing net over his shoulder.

Tanveer runs all the way down the slope. Shahana groans. He'll probably be wheezing by the time they get there. But when she catches up with him at the little river, Tanveer is happily up to his knees in the water. They are too close to the big river for Shahana's comfort; she can see the razor wire of the Line of Control fence looming above the riverbank.

Tanveer shouts over the noise of the water. 'I can see one! It's shining – a big rainbow trout.'

Nana-ji taught Tanveer how to catch fish. Shahana

watches the net fly through the air as he throws it just as Nana-ji used to.

She blinks as Tanveer calls out, 'I have it! Help me, Shahji.'

Shahana grabs one side of the net and pushes it underwater to meet his hands, which are holding the other side. Even though the little river is a tributary and not as fast as the blue Neelum, the water is cold and strong, and she has to dig her feet into the dirt and pebbles to keep upright. They drag the net and the fish onto the stony bank.

'How beautiful he is,' Tanveer says.

'If we take anything from its natural environment it will lose its shine and joy.' It is something their mother said. Shahana likes repeating things her mother told her; it makes her feel she is taking good care of Tanveer.

'Yes, but we have need of you, King Trout.' Tanveer sits cross-legged beside it on the grass and lets it die naturally, the way Nana-ji said. He murmurs, 'Bismillah, in the name of God,' even though he doesn't have to for a fish. Shahana hands him the cloth bag. The fish will feed them for a few days at least.

They make their way back up the slope under the chinar trees, their broad three-pointed leaves shining orange and red, like silken flames. The forest looks as if it is on fire. Shahana breathes in the fresh sharpness of the fir trees nearby. Tanveer carries the fish and he starts to tell a story. 'We are children of the Moghul emperor and we have just been fishing in the royal lake. Now we glide home on the lake in a beautiful shikara.

My oar is shaped like a heart and I row between the water gardens, when all of a sudden the boat—'

A dog barks, then another. Shahana and Tanveer climb quickly to keep away from the wild dogs. Tanveer looks down to the little river and beyond it, to the Neelum. 'Those dogs…'

'Do not worry,' Shahana says. 'They won't catch us up here.' She hopes her words hold true.

'Shahji, look, it's a boy. By the big river.'

Shahana stops and shades her eyes. How can Tanveer see that far?

'A boy?'

'He's not fighting the dogs.'

Shahana sees a shape lying on the ground and wonders if the boy is dead. A wave of nausea washes over her. 'What can we do? We cannot help him.' She begins to climb again.

'We have to, Shahji. What if it was Irfan? Or Abu?'

She stares at Tanveer in shock. He hardly ever mentions their father or brother. He is standing with his legs apart like a man.

She hesitates; always she has tried to avoid going near the Neelum. 'Teik hai, okay. We shall see what we can do, but you keep behind me. I do not want you bitten by a wild dog. What if they have the dog sickness?'

'Maybe we can throw the net over them,' Tanveer ventures, sounding like a young boy again.

'That will just make them angry.' She picks up a stick and leans on it to test its strength. 'This should do.'

Tanveer bites his lip. 'You will be careful?'

'Certainly, and you keep hold of that fish.' She hopes the dogs don't smell it.

There are five dogs circling the body. They look like wolves, dark, though one is yellow. Shahana suspects they are Bakarwal dogs, left behind when the nomads moved their sheep and goats away from the fighting. One dog rushes to the body and worries it; another barks for its turn. How can she help? They sound so fierce. She tries not to look at the body. It only makes her think of that other time. Is Tanveer remembering it too?

'Tanveer, fetch some stones from the river. Show me how far you can throw them.'

Shahana waits until Tanveer reaches the river and collects some stones from the shore. Then he takes a run-up, like a cricketer. The first stone lands wide. The next produces a yelp, then a growl.

'Keep throwing,' Shahana shouts, then she charges down the slope screaming and holding the stick high. When she reaches the dogs only three remain. She hits one and it retreats to a safe distance but one of Tanveer's stones chases it further. Then another one runs. The yellow dog bares its teeth and holds its ground but Shahana whacks it over the head. The stick breaks. Shahana stands motionless; the dog snarls and edges closer. Then *zing*, a stone thumps into its chest, and another. With a yelp, the dog jumps away.

Shahana has seen enough corpses to know the boy doesn't have the look of death. She yells for Tanveer. 'Jaldi, quickly, we have to take him before they come back.' Two of the dogs are a long way off, but they are circling in the manner of wolves planning to sneak up on their prey.

'Bring the net,' Shahana cries.

Tanveer spreads it on the ground next to the boy and she lays her woollen shawl over it. They manage to roll the boy so the net and shawl are under him. 'Now, pull!'

It is not easy. Maybe down the slope they could have easily dragged a dead weight like the boy, but not uphill. At least once they are across the stony riverbank, the grass is smooth. The first time they take a rest, two of the dogs are close behind them; one is the yellow dog that held its ground by the river. Shahana can see the rushing Neelum River and the fence of the Line of Control, where the river changes direction. 'Pull! Pull, Tanveer!'

The yellow dog snarls at the net. It is too close to the boy's feet; he isn't wearing shoes. Shahana shouts at the dog but this does no good. It edges closer, snarling. It bares its teeth at Shahana but she doesn't know who it will attack first.

Just then a single shot rings out. Shahana drops the net and grabs Tanveer. She was crazy to say they could come near the big river. What was she thinking? Even if the dogs don't attack them, they will be shot.

Tanveer struggles in her grip. 'Shahji, it's okay, look!'

Shahana kneels up to check. It is true – the yellow dog is dead and the other has gone. The threat has disappeared.

'A soldier must have helped us,' Tanveer says.

Shahana doesn't think so. Perhaps a sniper was aiming for them and hit the dog instead. But there is no need to worry Tanveer; she forces herself to smile. 'Alhamdulillah, praise be to God.'

Then she vomits on the grass.

Chapter 4

It takes all morning, with many rests, to haul the boy home. 'Help me drag him up to the door,' Shahana says. This will be the hardest part yet. Rani edges closer and nuzzles the boy's shalwar, but Tanveer shoos her away. A few centimetres at a time they pull the boy up the log ramp.

Shahana slips inside and lays the cotton mattress from their charpoy onto the floor, then they drag the boy in and roll him onto it. She puts a blanket on their string bed for them to sleep on that night. At least they have Nana-ji's quilt. Shahana takes it out of the clothes trunk and lays it over the boy.

'Get some water, Tanveer.' He races to the spring with a bucket while Shahana brings the fire to life in the hollow in the dirt floor. When Tanveer returns she fills the samovar with water and puts live coals in its central chimney to heat it. She takes water in a cup to the boy and urges him to drink, but his mouth is slack.

'At least we can keep him warm,' Tanveer says. He

squats beside the boy on the namdah, the felt rug Shahana has embroidered with wool, and they both watch him. Tanveer looks wistful but Shahana is frowning. Tanveer was right about Irfan. The boy looks about fifteen – the same age their brother was when they saw him last, that day he was walking her to school. She closes her eyes a moment. The boy has pale skin like their family, too. Maybe he is from Azad Kashmir and has just got lost. But why is he hurt? Perhaps he fell in the river, or hit his head and was washed up. She checks his head but there is no injury. When she lifts his qameez, there is no blood on his body. Only on his leg there is a wound where the dogs nipped him.

When the water is boiled she washes the boy's face then rolls up his shalwar and cleans the gash on his leg. She puts salt on it and binds it with a clean rag. She doesn't know what else to do. There is no medicine in their house except the special tablets and spray for Tanveer in case his breathing grows raspy.

'What if the dog that bit him was sick?' Tanveer whispers, as if the boy can hear him.

'Then we cannot help him,' she murmurs.

'Shahji,' Tanveer says quietly. 'The net is ripped.' He doesn't say what Shahana is thinking. *How will we catch fish with a torn net?*

Shahana tries to sound brave for her brother. 'I will repair it,' she says.

Tanveer slips out to collect firewood and fallen chinar leaves. 'Ao, come, Rani.' He takes her with him so she can carry the wood in a basket on her back, like a horse. Shahana picks up her embroidery in a daze, forgetting to remind him to stay nearby. She must do it, whether she feels like it or not, so they can buy food, and string to fix the net. Her grandfather said that the quality of stitching does not differ between the times you feel joy in your work and when you don't. It is advice that has helped her through many a hard week's labour.

While she stitches, she broods. Who is the boy? And if he gets better what will she do with him? If Irfan or her parents were alive they would know what to do. She can't take him to Aunty Rabia, for she won't open her door. Nor can she take him to Mr Nadir. He'd probably sell the boy to a factory. But she mustn't keep him in the house. What if someone found out she had an unrelated male staying with them? They would think she had a relationship with him and that is haram, forbidden.

—o—o—o—

The setting sun casts a shadow from the mountains Sharda and Nardi, and Shahana lights the oil lamp. It is cooler in the evenings now, but the gas bottle ran out a month after Nana-ji died and she has never had enough money to fill it. Many times she and Tanveer are cold at night, even with Nana-ji's quilt. She hopes the fire will warm the room enough for the boy.

She tries to put him out of her mind while she cuts up the fish for their curry and cooks it in the pan over the fire. She adds garlic, an onion, cumin, cinnamon, salt, some aloo, potatoes, and yoghurt that she has made from Rani's milk. If only she had some tamarind; her mother often cooked fish in tamarind paste. She leaves the pan by the fire to keep warm while she boils the rice in the dekshi, the cooking pot. Trout is a special dish so she puts a tiny pinch of saffron in the rice to colour it. When she has no saffron she uses turmeric instead. Her mother always said to use food while you had it and God would provide more.

Shahana sighs; she can't forget the boy. If he had been able to walk she could have directed him to the village mosque. She and Tanveer can't take him anywhere else now; it was so much effort getting him to the house.

When the food is ready she calls Tanveer. Her tone is sharper than she wants it to be but she can't help it. Tanveer says 'bismillah' and they eat together. Tanveer sucks the fish's head. 'So tasty,' he says. 'Pity we can't give the boy some.' He stares over at the mattress with such yearning that Shahana is afraid for him. Even if the boy survives, he will not be the brother Tanveer longs for.

'We will feed him tomorrow,' she says. Her voice sounds firmer than she feels, for she thinks the boy will die in the night. His chest is barely moving. It was like that when she and Tanveer found their father, except they couldn't drag him to the house; she was only eleven, Tanveer seven. He was down by the Neelum River, near the suspension bridge that crosses to the other side. Some people could get a permit to walk to the middle of the bridge and meet relatives. But their father didn't want to stay on the bridge: he wanted to cross to the other side of Kashmir to sell his shawls. He didn't want to work for Mr Nadir anymore, not once Mr Nadir began using young boys to work for him through debt bondage.

They found their father in the evening lying in a pool of blood on the stones by the river. He must have managed to crawl back across the bridge. Whether he had been targeted or just in the line of fire they never knew. Shahana begged him to wake up. 'Abu, Abu-ji, don't leave us,' she cried, not knowing if he could hear her above the roar of the river. Tanveer cried too. When their father realised they were there, he stretched out a hand and touched them each on their heads; then his hand dropped. He didn't manage to say a word but he had given them a blessing. Some men carried him to Nana-ji's house so he could be washed ready for burial the next morning.

She hopes Tanveer will not be too upset if the boy dies. Although he rarely mentions Irfan, Shahana knows how much he misses him. She does too. There isn't a day when she doesn't think of Irfan and how much easier it would be if he were here looking after them. She sighs deeply. If the boy dies, she will just have to go to the village and ask a man to take him to the mosque. But will they believe that he had only just come?

That night, Shahana wakes from a dream of snarling dogs surrounding her, moaning and snapping at her legs. Tanveer is still asleep – she can hear his uneven breathing – but the snapping and moaning is in the room with her. She lights a candle and drops down beside the boy. He is rolling his head from side to side too fast, muttering words. Shahana scoops some water into a cup and tries to pour some down his throat. A little goes in his mouth and the rest spills onto the mattress. The night is not warm and yet he feels so hot to her touch. She tries cooling his face with a wet cloth, and the thrashing gradually stops. His eyes are shut but he says words Shahana doesn't understand. He says them louder and Shahana glances at Tanveer, hoping he doesn't wake.

She sings softly, *This is Paradise, the flower carpets and fresh rosebuds, the buds tie a knot in the heart.* It is a tune her mother sang. Shahana is not sure she has the words right but her mother said Emperor Jahangir wrote them in a poem. He thought Kashmir was Paradise.

The boy's breathing becomes deeper. She lays her hand on his chest and watches it rise and fall. Maybe he will survive after all. She climbs onto the charpoy with Tanveer. This will be different from her father and Irfan. She finds herself hoping the boy will not die, even though she will have more trouble than she first thought. This she knows because he is not from Azad Kashmir. He speaks a different language: a language from Jammu and Kashmir – the other side of the Line of Control.

Chapter 5

In the morning, the boy wakes shouting, his eyes clenched shut as if against some horror. He struggles to sit up, but falls back on the mattress. Shahana rushes to him. Have they rescued a mad boy? 'Chup, chup, quiet, you are safe.'

The boy throws out his arms and Shahana jumps back. 'Open your eyes. We will not hurt you.' She speaks in Pahari but it has no effect. She tries Urdu. 'You are safe.'

The boy quietens; his eyes open. They are grey like Irfan's, and Shahana's breath catches in her throat.

'Where are you from?' She blinks, as if to stop the memories.

The boy stares at Shahana and Tanveer. 'Who will you tell?'

Shahana snorts. 'Do you think we will be telling anyone about you?' She tries another question. 'Which language were you speaking in the night?'

The boy looks surprised. 'Koshur, Kashmiri.' He

adds, 'I am from a village in the Kashmir Valley. Not far from the LoC.'

Tanveer asks, 'What is your good name?'

The boy hesitates a moment, then says, 'Zahid Amir Kumar.'

'So you are Muslim, like us,' Tanveer says.

The boy tilts his head in affirmation.

'Why are you here?' Shahana asks.

Zahid's eyes flicker and a shadow falls across his face.

'What am I doing?' Shahana says quickly, sorry she asked. 'We must get you something to eat, some chai. Then you will feel better.'

Zahid manages to sit up and looks around the room. His face is pale, as if he will faint.

Shahana fills the samovar with water and tea leaves. Zahid lets out a small breath. 'I am looking for my father,' he says, as if Shahana has only just asked her question. 'He disappeared three years ago. We used to live in Srinagar then. My mother sat in a park every month with a sign in Angrezi, English, that said, "Where are our missing husbands and sons?"'

'Why in Angrezi?' Tanveer asks.

'The women wanted the world to know what was happening. Maybe a journalist would take a picture. But very few journalists came.'

Shahana thinks of Aunty Rabia. Does she wait for her husband to come home? Even to find out he died would be better for her. Then she would be the esteemed widow of a martyr.

Zahid continues. 'The Indian soldiers came in a van

and took him away. They would have interrogated him. They would have—' He breaks off as Shahana shakes her head and glances at Tanveer.

'What did the soldiers do?' Tanveer asks anyway.

With a measured glance at Shahana, Zahid says, 'They would have kept him in prison, perhaps.'

'Then you could visit him?'

'We don't know which one. Maybe they let him go.'

'Then he would have come home?'

Shahana can see the annoyance well up in Zahid's face and she shushes Tanveer. But Zahid answers him. 'I have seen men who have been interrogated. Sometimes they do not remember who they are.' Then he glances at Shahana and says, 'Sometimes they die. I just need to know.'

Tanveer is quiet, though Shahana can see he'd like to ask more questions. Even at his age he recognises sorrow, and there is no need to talk. Shahana does what her mother would have done: she cooks roti.

Zahid manages to swallow some of the warm bread and drink his chai. Shahana smiles at him. She won't be dressing a corpse anytime soon. Then her smile fades. It is strange how he has managed to cross the Line of Control.

It is Tanveer who asks what Shahana is thinking. 'So how did you cross over the LoC? There are mines between the two electric fences, and razor wire.'

Zahid answers too quickly and Shahana looks up from her chai. 'I came across the river.'

'The big river, the Neelum?' Shahana asks.

29

'We call it the Kishanganga.'

'So you can swim,' Tanveer says, awe in his tone. But Shahana knows it would take more than a strong swimmer to cross the Neelum. It would take a miracle.

'Not very well,' Zahid admits. 'The river pulled me under and spat me out. Where you found me,' he adds.

'You were fortunate,' Shahana says, thinking of her father. 'The river kills in more ways than drowning.'

'There are Indian and Pakistani soldiers,' Tanveer adds. 'Our father—' He stops himself, then asks, 'Why didn't they see you?'

'It was night-time, there was no moon,' Zahid says.

Shahana shoots him a swift glance. The soldiers see everything, even at night. Nana-ji told her they have motion sensors and thermal imaging devices that they carry with them in the dark. Their father was shot at night.

Zahid's eyes hold knowledge, and a certain wariness. 'Perhaps it is different travelling in this direction?' he says.

Shahana thinks that is possible. The Indian soldiers on the other side may have thought her father was a militant, but who would mind on this side if a jihadi militant returned home? Though she has heard that the army has been warned to watch out for terrorists. The problem is, whether a man is a militant or a terrorist depends on which side you are on. She glances at Zahid again. Anyone can see Zahid is not a militant. He looks just like a jawan, a teenaged boy.

—o—o—o—

Later, when both boys are asleep, Shahana opens Nana-ji's trunk and takes out his white embroidered cap and shoes. She kneels there, thinking, then carefully puts them back. What if Zahid is not just an innocent jawan? She would wait and see if he is worthy to wear Nana-ji's shoes.

Chapter 6

When Shahana wakes in the morning, Tanveer is gone. She peers over the edge of the charpoy. Zahid is not on the mattress either. Her heart beats like a drum and nausea rises before she realises she can't hear Rani's bell under the house. The milk is in a pot on the floor. The boys must be out finding firewood. Usually Tanveer is asking questions when she wakes. It is a peaceful feeling to wake alone.

She stretches and winces; her back aches this morning. She will have a wash in the spring. Who knows how long the weather will hold? She hasn't had a proper wash since Eid ul Fitr in the early autumn. There was no joy at Eid, no one to visit and share food with, though she tried to make it fun for Tanveer. At least they had fish to eat and prayed together.

She takes her soap and towel and a clean set of clothes. She has only a few outfits. She even unpicked one of Nana-ji's, managing to get an outfit for Tanveer out of it, too. It is a pity her mother's beautiful clothes burned in the fire.

The spring bubbles at her. A fowl, with a turquoise and gold head, fluffs up its feathers on a rock. She can't stop thinking about Tanveer. Have the boys gone together? Will Zahid watch out for him? She quickly peels off the shalwar she has worn and slept in for weeks, washes and dries her lower half, then pulls on a clean one. She does the same with her qameez. She untwists the plait at her back and shakes out her hair. As she puts her head under the water, she flinches – it is even colder on her head. Her head aches but she rubs the soap in and rinses it out. It would be good to have shampoo, but she has to keep her money for food and medicine. When she went to school her mother washed her hair every Friday with Gloss shampoo. After school she and Ayesha would pretend they were hairdressers, brushing each other's hair. Now, whenever Shahana combs her hair much of it is left on the comb.

She washes her dirty outfit in the spring, bangs it on a rock then spreads it on a bush to dry. She is plaiting her hair when the boys return with Rani.

Zahid is limping and Shahana feels a pang that he has no shoes. He helps Tanveer lift the basket of firewood from Rani's back. Normally women collect the firewood in baskets on their heads and men sew, but everything in their lives is upside down now.

Tanveer chats, but Zahid is quiet and pale. 'I showed Zahid where we catch the best fish.' He gives a little jump.

Shahana's hand stills on her plait. 'You went near the big river?'

'Not too close.' He grins at her.

Shahana frowns at Zahid. She can't decide if he is not strong enough yet to walk on the mountain or if something has upset him. She quickly finishes the plaiting and gathers her things together. 'Come inside,' she says. 'I will make roti for breakfast.'

Her comb slips out of her hand and Zahid picks it up. It is something Irfan would have done. 'Shukriya,' she murmurs her thanks. His kindness disturbs her; it would be easier if he weren't kind, easier to send him away. She knows he should leave as soon as he is well enough. *An unrelated male cannot stay in the house,* she imagines her mother warning her. But Shahana is not sure she wants him to leave – she hasn't seen Tanveer this happy for so long. The thought of her brother calms her. Tanveer will always be there; she and Zahid will never be alone.

'Did you milk Rani?' she asks Zahid as they walk along the logs up to the door. Tanveer still hasn't learned how.

He nods, and she thanks him again.

'Your house is built high,' he says. 'Our house in Srinagar was too, in case the lake flooded.'

'Ours is for the snow,' Shahana says. 'If we didn't build high with a space underneath the house, the snow would trap us for months.'

'Like Eskimos.' Zahid smiles.

Shahana stares at him. His teeth look white and even,

34

like her father's. Zahid looks almost a man. How can she possibly keep him there?

Tanveer's chatter brings her back to her surroundings. 'What are Eskimos?'

'People who live at the North Pole,' Zahid says. 'They live with snow all around them – not just on the top of a mountain.'

Tanveer's questions come thick and fast. Shahana fills the samovar, then cooks flatbread on the stones around the fire. Soon they will have to cut grass and dry it for the floor, before it gets much colder.

She glances over at the boys. 'Zahid,' she says when there is a lull in their conversation. 'When we go to the village you could wear a shawl over your face, wear my clothes.' She is thinking of the shalwar qameez she made from Nana-ji's outfit, though she suspects it won't fit him.

'No!' He stands, then pauses, as if catching his breath. 'I couldn't do that,' he says more quietly.

'You don't want to be seen, do you? You don't have any papers. People may think you are a fugitive.' She doesn't like the way her voice sounds, as though she doesn't believe him. But what if he lied?

His face whitens as if he is sick again. 'In that case,' he says, 'I will not go to the village.'

'Someone may come up here and see you.'

'Does everyone in this area know you?'

'Possibly.' *Now*, her mother scolds. *Now is the time to tell him to leave.*

'Zahid,' she says, then stops.

Tanveer catches on to the conversation. 'He can stay.' He says it loudly, as if Shahana is already telling Zahid to go, then turns to Zahid. 'You won't leave us?'

Zahid is quiet as he watches Shahana.

A knot of fear forms in Shahana's chest. He can't stay, but how can she send him away? Winter is close. An image of Nana-ji gasping for breath in the cold night lodges in her mind.

She sighs, ignoring the voices in her head. 'You can be our cousin from Muzaffarabad. We have some family there, though we've not seen them since we were small.'

'A brother might be better.' For a moment there is a playful glint in Zahid's eyes. It is not seemly for him to stay – *no, no*, her mother shouts – but they need him. Nana-ji died at the end of last winter and Shahana is not sure she can get through another without help.

'Everyone knows our brother is dead,' she says dully.

Zahid's expression changes. 'I am sorry. I didn't mean to upset you.'

Tanveer isn't daunted. 'You're just like him – that's why we want you to stay.'

Shahana takes the bread off the stones and lays it on tin plates. *It's not true*, she says to herself. Zahid is not 'just like' Irfan. His eyes are the same, his skin, too, but his nose is straighter, his hair darker.

The room is quiet while they eat. There is a little fish left and Shahana gives it to Zahid to help him grow stronger.

When he is finished Zahid looks as if he will collapse as he lies on the mattress. She should tell him to sleep under the house with Rani, but it will be cold. She'll wait until he is better.

'We can go up the mountain. We could catch game,' Zahid says slowly.

'And we can take our grandfather's rifle,' Tanveer says without looking at Shahana.

She presses her lips together. She has never wanted Tanveer to touch that rifle. Look at what has happened to them because of weapons. Nana-ji said the culture of the gun has replaced the Kashmiri culture of peace and tolerance. He called it Kashmiriyat.

'The rifle will only be used to obtain food, to give us life.' Zahid is leaning on his elbow, his gaze on Shahana, and she knows Tanveer has talked of the rifle.

What if she gives Zahid the rifle and he runs off, or shoots Tanveer? 'No,' she says.

There is a silence that even Tanveer doesn't break.

Shahana explains, 'You must understand – we have had much trouble. We are the only ones left in our family.'

The shadow fills Zahid's face again and Shahana is ashamed of her distrust. Everyone has had trouble. She tries to say she is sorry, that she knows Zahid must have sorrow too, but he stops her.

'Shahana, you have taken me into your home, you have fed me. While I am here I will be your family. I will be like a brother to you and to Veer.'

Veer? Shahana starts at the nickname. When did they become so close?

37

Tanveer jumps up and shouts. 'Alhamdulillah, praise be to God.'

Shahana doesn't share his jubilation, for she has caught the words Tanveer has missed. *While I am here.*

Chapter 7

They climb the slope; more trees have burst into fire. Shahana loves the trees aflame but dreads what will follow. The leaves are falling; soon winter will be here.

Tanveer carries the bag they use to put fish in. Shahana has her backpack with her embroidery in it. While the boys chase a wild musk goat or hare she must sit and get some work done or she will never make enough money for all three of them.

Tanveer runs ahead and Zahid calls him back before Shahana can. 'Hoi, Veer, we don't want to frighten off our khana, our food.'

Shahana waits under a chinar tree and takes out her sewing. Chinar trees are special to their valley – the Moghul emperors planted them. She can see the boys moving further up the mountain.

Zahid seems so well now, she thinks. He hardly limps and there is no sign of the dog sickness, no sudden bursts of anger or drooling, though he argued with her before they left about the rifle. Tanveer took his side. 'How will we catch prey without a gun, Shahji?' he complained.

She hears a shot and stops sewing. Never will she get used to that sound. Was it a soldier? She quickly puts away her work and waits, but the boys don't return. Even when she stands she can't see them. She hears a man's shout further away. What has happened? Just as she starts up the slope, the boys come rushing down.

'Run!' Zahid says without stopping.

'What is it?' she asks.

'Jaldi ao, come quickly.'

Soon they reach thick bushes. They burrow under them and catch their breath.

'What did you see?' Shahana asks Tanveer.

'Militants.'

Shahana's whole body stiffens, but the thumping in her chest is loud and fast. Militants are not always evil men, but it was militants who caused the trouble when Irfan and their mother died. Those militants had left. A new group must have come to train in the mountains.

'What did they look like?' she asks, trying to ignore the galloping in her chest.

'They had turbans and full beards like Pakistani tribal men,' Tanveer says.

Shahana glances at Zahid. He has said nothing about the militants. There is sweat on the hairs of his young moustache. He is pale and pulls in his breath like Tanveer does when he has a breathing attack.

'Zahid? Are you hurt?' she asks. Maybe he is not as well as she thought.

He is shaking and she moves closer.

'Did they shoot at you?' Was that the shot she heard?

'No,' Tanveer says. He also is watching Zahid.

Finally Zahid says, 'I can't let them see me.' His voice sounds as if it's been stretched too far.

'Why?' Shahana asks. 'Surely they won't shoot children?'

'They'll know I am from across the LoC.'

'How can they know this? You look like us.'

Zahid stares at her miserably and she catches her tongue between her teeth. She knows there is something he is not saying; she has known it since that first night.

'Come,' she says then. 'They are not following.'

Tanveer has a dead hare in his bag. 'I ran it down,' he says, displaying it proudly when they reach the house. Shahana can see that its blood has been drained in the proper way. 'It would have been easier with the rifle,' Tanveer adds, and Shahana can hear the reproach in his tone.

She doesn't comment but catches Zahid glancing at her as he takes out his knife. They watch Zahid skin the hare, remove the organs and cut it into pieces. Then Shahana takes the meat inside.

While she cooks it in a pot over the fire with onions and spices, thoughts crowd her mind like monkeys chattering. Is it safe to let Zahid stay with them? She knows if she asks him, he will shut his mouth. She will have to be patient, but she will watch him carefully.

When she lights the lamp the boys tie up Rani under the house and come inside.

'Mmm,' Tanveer says. 'This hare is tasty.' He seems to have forgotten the run down the slope to safety, or perhaps he has learned Shahana's trick of shutting unpleasant things out. She thinks of the stone princess, still etched into the mountain, and sighs. She knows what it feels like to be made of stone. If only stone held firm against fear.

Regardless of her concerns about Zahid, Shahana decides she must thank him. It is the first time they have had meat since Nana-ji died. She says shukriya, but he just inclines his head. She watches him as he eats; he glances up at her but looks away. His fear is palpable. What isn't he telling her? That the militants could hurt them? She knows that already.

—o—o—o—

When Tanveer has fallen asleep, Shahana takes out the pheran and the green thread and sits by the lamp. It is so cold at night now that she gets up to scoop coals from the fire and puts them in a clay pot inside a basket. Zahid watches her.

'You use kangris, fire pots, also?'

Shahana nods. 'We always have. This one is my grandfather's. Did you need them in Srinagar?'

'It gets cold there as well – snow everywhere. The lake freezes.'

Shahana puts the kangri beside her, then sits on a cushion. Zahid still looks pale; she hesitates, then holds out a cushion to him. 'Come, sit by the kangri, you will be cold otherwise.'

'My mother always put her kangri under her pheran, even when she was working in our vegetable garden.'

'We do this too.' Shahana's answers are short. She is not sure what to say to Zahid when there is such a large valley between them. She waits to see if he will say what is troubling him. Everything important has to be waited for.

Shahana has stitched half of the forest on the neck of the pheran when Zahid finally says, 'The militants are causing trouble in Kashmir.'

'Aren't they there to help you gain your azadi, your freedom?'

'So they say. But before they came we only had to watch out for the soldiers and our own militants. We call our national militants freedom fighters. Many are peaceful groups that only want freedom from India. But the militants from Pakistan and beyond are fierce and don't warn civilians they will fight the army in the streets.'

Shahana understands the bitterness so she says nothing. If she knew the soldiers and militants were fighting the day Irfan took her to school she would have stayed home and Irfan and her mother would still be alive.

'Now we have to watch three ways,' Zahid continues. 'The jihadi militants from Pakistan are zealous and don't know us. They want to change our ways. They try to beat the soldiers back to India and don't care if civilians get hurt. They only care about their cause. Freedom, they say.' He grunts. 'What worth is freedom if we are all dead?'

43

'You can all come here to Azad Kashmir. Many refugees from Jammu and Kashmir have come to Muzaffarabad.'

'The Indian soldiers call this place Pakistani-occupied Kashmir.'

'We are not Pakistanis,' she hisses. 'We are a state with our own president.'

'But you are under the sovereignty of Pakistan.'

'We are all Kashmiris. It was all meant to be part of Azad Kashmir in the beginning.'

'That's not true.' Zahid says it too loudly and Tanveer rolls over on the charpoy.

'Chup se, quietly,' Shahana whispers.

'We were always free,' Zahid says softly but firmly. 'We were a state with a maharajah, never part of India to be handed over to Pakistan at Partition or to China. When India and Kashmir were divided into Hindu India and Muslim Pakistan in 1947 the two states went to war to control Kashmir. Since then, this conflict hasn't stopped.'

Shahana has not heard all this before. She would rather have peace, whatever it took. Then there would be no fighting, no fear. They could go to school and there would be justice. Is it possible to have both peace and freedom?

'We are all Muslims,' she says. 'We should live together.' Would that bring peace?

'All religions lived together well enough in Kashmir before Partition. My best friend was a Hindu but they had to flee because of the trouble from the militants.'

Zahid pauses. 'Everyone has a view about Kashmir – India, Pakistan, the rest of the world. It is like two children tugging both ends of a doll – soon it will tear apart.' He is quiet for a while, watching Shahana's needle, then he says, 'Do you know the LoC cuts through some people's land?'

Shahana shakes her head.

'One family I know eat in "Indian" Kashmir and grow their vegetables in "Pakistani" Kashmir.'

'It's Azad Kashmir.' Shahana is not used to hearing the passion she senses in Zahid's tone. Nor can she understand why Kashmir should be divided – it is too confusing.

He ignores the correction. 'We just want the Indian army to go. With the curfew, people can't even get their sick children to the doctor. My grandmother said there was peace and tolerance sixty years ago. When she was young she marched in the women's army in Red Square in Srinagar, but they carried wooden guns. Now the kids have a different alphabet. A for army, B for bullet, C for curfew and D for dead.' He sighs. 'I cannot tell these things in the day.'

Shahana nods over her stitching. The day is to enjoy, to live, not to remember. Besides, she is glad they are having this conversation when Tanveer is asleep.

'The militants make boys into fighters.'

Her needle stills. Is this why Zahid was running from the militants on the mountain? 'Was your father a freedom fighter?' she asks. Maybe that is why he wants to use the rifle.

Zahid's mouth twists into a bitter smile. 'No, but the Indian soldiers thought he was. He marched for freedom. That is all he did, but the next day they took him away.' He pauses and then whispers, 'Kashmir used to be Paradise, now it is burning, now it is Jahanam, hell.'

Suddenly Zahid stops talking of war as if he has turned off a lamp. 'How did you learn to stitch so well?' Shahana can hear the real question in his tone: *You're a girl; how come you can sew?*

'My grandfather. He realised I could stitch better than my father and so he taught me the patterns. Abu bought pashmina shawls and Nana-ji and I stitched them. Then Abu sold them.' She stopped to bite a thread. 'My mother had a sewing machine. She taught girls and women how to sew and make patterns. When I was too young to stitch she had a weaving loom, too. That was when she wove the shawls Nana-ji embroidered. It took six months to complete one.'

She looks across at Zahid. 'What is your talent?'

'I used to play a reed flute at home.'

Shahana crawls across to Nana-ji's trunk and takes out a long whistle made of wood. 'Like this?'

Zahid holds it, putting his fingers over the holes. 'Ji.' He plays a few notes.

Shahana listens to the haunting tones, entranced as Zahid plays a rag, an old tune. Even Nana-ji didn't play as well as Zahid does.

When he finishes she goes back to Nana-ji's trunk and takes out his shoes and white cap. 'You will need these,' she says.

He accepts them as if he understands how hard it is for her. He tilts his head in thanks. She is struck by how similar they are, even though they live on opposite sides of the Line of Control.

'Shahana, I need to start sleeping under the house.'

She doesn't argue; he is getting better and it is the correct thing to do. For him to sleep inside with her is haram.

Then he says quietly, 'I will need the rifle – to protect us all.'

She feels a void open inside her as though she is hanging on to a cliff and is losing her grip. She looks at Zahid and for a moment sees just a teenage boy.

She nods just once.

Chapter 8

In the morning Shahana wakes early, prays and takes the pots out to the stream to wash. There is a mist and the air is icy. She tightens her shawl around her. Soon she will need to start wearing her pheran.

Tanveer follows her out with the bucket to milk Rani. Zahid is already there. Shahana watches as Zahid shows Tanveer how to milk the goat. Some milk squirts in Tanveer's eye and he giggles.

'Don't waste the milk,' she scolds, but she is happy. After their conversation the night before, Zahid feels almost like a brother. She is not sure if he has explained everything about himself, and she knows her mother would send him away, but Tanveer would never forgive her if she didn't let Zahid stay. She watches his hands guide Tanveer's, and wonders if he too has a young brother.

After breakfast Shahana sends Tanveer to fetch the rifle from behind the door for Zahid. She can feel the fear curling around her neck.

'Hoi, Veer, never point it at anyone.' Zahid takes it from him and inspects it. He pulls a lever. 'Hmm, it is old, but a good one, a Lee Enfield. It needs cleaning.' He looks up at Shahana. 'Is there a cloth I can use? Hot water and soap? Oil?'

Tanveer gets the water and soap. Shahana takes a soft rag from Nana-ji's trunk and a small bottle of sewing-machine oil. It is Shahana's dream to have a sewing machine. The oil has always made her feel as if one day the dream will happen: she will be able to make clothes and have enough money to live. She hands the dream to Zahid. He smiles up at her but the collar of dread circling her throat does not loosen. She watches him work with the soapy hot water and can't stop herself from wondering how he learned to clean a rifle.

She busies herself packing the pheran and the left-over green thread into her backpack. Zahid fell asleep before her in the night but she managed to stay awake to finish the sewing. She is pleased with her work and hopes Mr Nadir will be too. She has always wondered what it would be like to stitch with silver thread.

This time she leaves Tanveer at home with Zahid, who has promised to care for him. To take Tanveer with her to Mr Nadir would be a bigger worry. 'Be careful,' she says to Tanveer. 'Stay close to home.'

Zahid slings the Lee Enfield over his shoulder. He does this too easily and Shahana's stomach tightens. She hopes she has done the right thing. As she walks past the spring he stands to watch her go, looking like a brother who knows he should accompany his sister to keep her safe. But Shahana wouldn't have let him go with her. Even though there are no police in their village he could still get into trouble, and so could she. And what would happen to Tanveer then?

She is not used to walking alone. She hears a noise and swings around but it is only the breeze in the trees knocking more leaves to the ground. They crackle as she walks through them. She passes Aunty Rabia's house. No one is outside, but that is not unusual.

Shahana reaches Mr Nadir's shop and, once inside, takes out the pheran. Has it only been a few weeks since she was here? So much has happened. She takes a deep breath as Mr Nadir comes out of the other room. She can hear the click clack of the carpet loom and imagines the little boys who work it – boys who may never see their homes again, little slaves forced to do whatever Mr Nadir asks. She shivers, glad she hasn't brought Tanveer.

Every time Mr Nadir inspects her work Shahana feels she is having a numbers test with her father. She used to hate those. Sometimes she didn't hear all the numbers that needed to be added together.

'Hmm.' Mr Nadir holds the pheran close to his face, then lowers it again and stares at her.

Shahana shifts on her feet. She is always uncomfortable under his scrutiny. He is frowning. What is he thinking? Hasn't she sewn well enough? She has tried to do such tiny stitches.

'It is not seemly,' he says at last.

Shahana almost falls, but clutches the counter. How has he found out about Zahid?

Mr Nadir goes on. 'You stitch beautifully, even better than most men, but it is not seemly.'

Shahana lets a breath escape. It is only the embroidery.

'You need to be married.'

She stills herself, like a hare in the forest scenting the air for danger.

'There are militants in the area again. It is not safe for you.'

'Will they not fight the Indian soldiers across the LoC?' she ventures, thinking of Zahid's words.

'Ji, that is their plan, but you have no husband to protect you while they train here.'

Shahana stares at Mr Nadir. 'Protect?' she whispers.

Mr Nadir smiles, but it isn't playful like Zahid's when he suggested he be her brother. 'Do you know what jihadis do to girls like you? They will take you away to make more militants.'

Shahana isn't sure she understands, for Mr Nadir is leering at her now.

'I know a man,' he says, 'who needs a nice young wife. How old are you now?'

Shahana makes herself speak. 'Too young, janab, too young for marriage.' A husband will feed her, clothe her and protect her, but he won't look after Tanveer. And what is the man like? If he is like Mr Nadir she will say no. Then her stomach tightens. Could Mr Nadir force her to marry? There is no one to speak for her. She can't produce Zahid as a brother. Mr Nadir will know he is not. Probably he will also know he is not her cousin.

The horror must show on her face for Mr Nadir nods in satisfaction. 'You may well be afraid, my girl. It is a good offer, so you should think about it. Your little brother can go to an orphanage or stay here with me and work on the loom. He will be well looked after. Think of me as a father – I will speak for you.'

Shahana shudders. Mr Nadir is nothing like her father. If only he were still alive. He was tall with a beard. Maybe that is why the Indian soldiers thought he was a Pakistani militant. Her father was different from other men in the village. He taught himself to read. He didn't think men should fight for their religion or kill others because they were different. He kept these ideas in the family but Nana-ji agreed with him. That was why Nana-ji chose him to marry his educated daughter.

'In the meantime,' Mr Nadir is saying, 'you can use silver thread on the next pheran. Be careful not to lose any thread or use too much. I will not give you more. It is expensive – pure silver.'

Shahana is so shocked by Mr Nadir's words of marriage and carpet looms she can't feel the joy of using silver thread. She has kept Tanveer safe all year, and he wouldn't be safe with Mr Nadir at all.

'Remember my offer. If your husband doesn't mind you can still work for me.'

'I do not wish to marry but thank you for your concern, janab.' It is politeness only. She doesn't know if Mr Nadir cares for her at all.

He sneers. 'You act so proud, just like your father. But you will be humbled. You will be glad to accept when winter is here.'

She takes the money he is holding between his two fingers, picks up her bag and backs out the door. Winter is harsh. Nana-ji said his mother called winter the three sisters. The first sister is the first forty days of winter, the second sister is the next twenty days. And the last and cruellest sister is the final ten days of winter. Nana-ji was weakened by the days that had gone before and it was the third sister that killed him.

Shahana's thoughts are wobbling all over the place. She drags herself to Mr Pervaiz's stall and takes so long to decide which vegetables to buy that he asks, 'Are you well, Shahana?'

She tilts her head.

'You look as though you've had a shock. Where is Tanveer?'

'He is home, janab.'

'Home? You never leave him alone.'

'He is getting older, more sensible.'

'Be careful, there are jihadis in the mountains now. They are not from here and they don't know our ways. All they know is to kill, and how to steal boys to train them into militants.'

'Girls, too?' Shahana doesn't know why she says it; maybe to check if Mr Nadir's story is true.

Mr Pervaiz's face changes. 'Only boys, but you be careful too.' He clicks his tongue. 'You need a mother, Shahana.'

She feels like saying she is a mother herself, but then she remembers the net.

'Do you have string?'

'What is it for?'

'The net. It got damaged.' She nibbles at her lip. She can't tell him how it got damaged. Are they even allowed to fish?

Mr Pervaiz takes down some green string. It shines like plastic. 'This will be best for the net.' Then he says, 'Shahana, I know your grandfather used to fish in the river, but be careful. There are rules about such things these days. Don't let anyone see you.'

Shahana buys more vegetables than usual. If Mr Pervaiz notices, he doesn't comment.

Then she thinks of Zahid and his mother's vegetable garden. 'Janab, do you have any seeds for vegetables?'

Mr Pervaiz frowns at her. 'Your family has never grown vegetables. Your grandfather only grew roses.'

'These are hard times, janab. I must try everything.' Then she says something Nana-ji used to say. 'Breaking water nuts on someone's head to eat is difficult.'

Mr Pervaiz chuckles and puts a few seeds in a small brown paper bag. 'Here, you can have these. They are saag, spinach. They grow in late autumn, though it might be too late now. You can try if you like. Shahana...' He hesitates as though he has difficult words to say. 'Have you ever thought of the orphanage? There are good ones now. There's a safe village for the refugees from across the LoC. They are orphans of the war. Like you,' he adds gently.

Shahana stares at him, blinking back tears. First Mr Nadir and now Mr Pervaiz. What is happening today?

'I am sorry to mention it, Shahana. I just worry about you on the mountain alone.'

'We are doing well, janab.' She tries to smile as she picks up her backpack. 'Shukriya.'

—o—o—o—

Shahana slows as she sees the shiny roof of Aunty Rabia's house. Then she stops. She walks up the wooden steps to the door and calls out, 'Aunty Rabia, assalamu alaikum. Ayesha, are you there?' There is a bag of vegetables by the door and the window is shut but Shahana hears a scuffle inside. She doesn't know what she can say that won't sound as if she is begging. She wants to plead, *I need you to help me. Please tell me what to do.* But all she says is, 'Khuda hafiz, may God be your protector.'

She waits a moment longer, her forehead resting on the door, but nothing happens. She walks down to the road. When she looks back, the door is ajar. Ayesha is picking up the vegetables. Even though Ayesha is looking at her, still she shuts the door, but she does it slowly. Shahana thinks about Ayesha's look. It isn't angry; it's a 'please understand' kind of look.

Shahana walks home strangely content. It is the first time in years that she and Ayesha have exchanged a glance. The first time in two years that she has seen their open door.

Chapter 9

When Shahana arrives home the boys are gone. So are Rani and the Lee Enfield. She purses her lips. Zahid doesn't seem to go anywhere without the rifle. She sweeps the house on her haunches with the hand broom, as her mother did, and makes dough for bread in the morning. Then she takes her scissors, the string and a bagging needle and goes under the house to start work on the net. She knots lengths of the green string over the holes. The string is thick and rope-like. She hopes the fish won't notice the shine on it. Nana-ji said anything strange in the water could scare them away.

She works quickly and has finished by the time Tanveer and Zahid come back with a basket of firewood. Tanveer unloads it to stack under the house while Rani tries to eat the net.

'No, Rani.' Shahana shoos her away.

Zahid squats beside Shahana. 'You are very skilful.'

'We are a family of stitchers.'

'Of nets, also?'

Shahana shrugs. 'Stitching is the same wherever you do it.' She cuts the final threads from the knots. The net looks as strong as ever.

Tanveer says to Zahid, 'We'll catch a fish in the morning.'

Shahana suspects Tanveer wants to show Zahid how well he can fish. She reaches into her pocket and hands Zahid the small paper bag.

He opens it. 'Saag seeds.' He looks up at the sky. 'It may be too late, but if we plant them in a sheltered place they may survive.'

Zahid takes Tanveer to a warm patch of ground near the house and gives him the spade Nana-ji used for snow. 'Dig,' he says, just like an older brother.

Shahana smiles at them. It is freeing to have someone else do things with Tanveer. She sits in the sun with the silver thread. The sun catches its facets and shines in her eyes. Pure silver. How she has wanted to work with silver. Will she ever get to embroider with gold? Wedding dupattas all have gold thread around the edges. Maybe Mr Nadir will give her gold next. But the thought of Mr Nadir and wedding dupattas wipes away her joy. The sooner she finishes, the sooner she will have to see Mr Nadir. What if he speaks of marriage again? What will she do? This house of Nana-ji's is theirs now – hers and Tanveer's. It is not as grand as Aunty Rabia's with her tin roof, two rooms and window, but as Nana-ji always said, the sparrow feels comfortable upon the thorn bush. This part of the forest feels like their country. How can she leave it? Mr Nadir didn't say where the man comes from. What if he lives far away? If only she could make money some other way and never see Mr Nadir again.

She threads the needle and watches how the silver thread sparkles as she pulls it through the pheran. Her mother's voice plays in her head. *Do not worry, the one who worries a lot rots. Enjoy the moment.* Did she worry as a child? Is that why she can remember her mother saying this? What would her mother say now? There is so much more to worry about.

Shahana loses herself in stitching the winter branches of the chinar trees and the leaves lying on the ground in patterns – pure silver, just like snow in the sunlight. She shivers as a wind springs up, straight from the snow on the mountains.

When the boys have finished planting Shahana packs up her sewing and goes inside to heat the dhal and bread.

◦–◦–◦

The next morning the boys take the net. They go early, so Shahana milks Rani and carries the bucket inside. When she emerges with her sewing there is a young man standing outside, petting Rani. Shahana stands very still by the door and carefully lifts her shawl over her head, but he has seen her. He looks like a militant; he carries a gun, an AK47 Kalashnikov, and wears a turban. He doesn't wear a vest, just a plain shawl, like a blanket, not like Kashmiri clothes at all.

'I heard your goat,' he says.

Her heart thumps; he must be a militant. She has never seen one this close. When he lifts his head she sees he is the age Irfan would be now. She berates herself for seeing Irfan in every stranger.

'What do you want?' she asks in Urdu, wishing her voice didn't waver.

'I want some milk. I will pay you.'

She dares to argue. 'I need the milk for my little brother. I cannot give milk every day.'

'I won't come every day.'

Shahana senses he won't leave without the milk. Will he hurt her if she refuses? She wants him gone before the boys return so she disappears inside, leaves her sewing on the charpoy, and pours some milk into an old Sprite bottle. Her hands are shaking so much she spills some. She walks halfway down the logs and stretches out an arm so the man can take the bottle, then she retreats up the logs again. He doesn't move, yet she can't relax.

'How many brothers and sisters do you have?' he asks.

Shahana thinks carefully. Is he asking for information? Or is he just being polite? What if he returns to take Zahid and Tanveer for fighters? How young do they take them?

She tells the truth. 'Two brothers. One died.'

'I am sorry to hear one died. How old are the other two?'

She lets him believe she has two brothers left. 'One is nine years.' Too young, she feels like shouting. 'The other is' – she hesitates – 'fifteen.' She is not sure how old Zahid is. There is so much about him she doesn't know.

Suddenly she realises what she must do. 'Janab, if you see them in the forest can you please protect them?' She suspects this young man is Pukhtun, from the same tribe as her father's mother. They protect orphans and live by a code of honour; once you ask them for protection and hospitality they will not kill you.

He hardly pauses. 'Zarur, certainly.' He hands her five rupees. 'I am sure you can use this.'

It is almost as much as Mr Nadir gives her. The young man doesn't smile. Shahana's father said the men in his mother's family rarely smile at strangers, and especially not at girls who are almost women.

'Shukriya.'

'You speak Urdu?' he asks, even though he can hear she can. But she knows why he is asking: only people who have gone to school speak Urdu.

'Ji, janab, as well as Pahari.' Then she adds, 'My grandmother spoke Pukhtu.'

His eyes glisten for a moment and she thinks he will smile, but he keeps control of his face. 'Khuda hafiz, may God be your protector,' he says formally with a slight nod. He gives Rani one last pat and strides off. Rani bleats and starts after him until Shahana calls her back.

Now what is she to do? Relief that he left without hurting her makes her legs weak. She slides down the wall onto the logs outside the door. If she tells Zahid, he will ask everything and find out what she has told. But what if she doesn't warn him, and then the militants come to take the boys away? Was Mr Pervaiz telling the truth about that? The young man didn't take her away as Mr Nadir had warned.

If she tells Zahid, he will leave. She knows this as certainly as she knows that winter will enclose them. Maybe the young man is just lonely for his family and wants milk to remind him of home. Maybe it is only milk that he wants.

Shahana is too troubled to concentrate on her sewing so she goes inside and packs it into her backpack. She walks to the door, looks out, then walks back to the bed. She does this many times and then she decides.

She will try to speak with Ayesha.

Chapter 10

Shahana walks slowly up the steps to Aunty Rabia's door. She calls out, but there is no sound from inside. Why did she think today would be any different? Because she saw Ayesha at the door? Because Ayesha had looked at her for a long time? It had meant nothing after all. Shahana returns to the road and heads towards the log bridge. How foolish she was to come.

'Shahana!'

Shahana doesn't hear her name at first.

'Wait! Shahana...'

She turns. Ayesha is hurrying after her as quickly as decorum will allow. She is wearing a black burqa but she has the veil up. Shahana runs towards her. Just before they hug, they stop and stare at each other's faces. It has been so long. Shahana kisses Ayesha on both sides of her face.

Ayesha says, 'I didn't think you would want to speak to me again.'

'Why?'

'Because of our trouble. Your father was well respected and now is a martyr, while people say bad things about mine. They say he ran away.'

'Do you think my parents would mind about that?'

Ayesha shook her head miserably. 'My mother is so unwell. She is the one who doesn't understand.'

'Does she know you are here?'

'Nay, she is resting so I haven't long. When she wakes she will expect me to be there, or she will...' she hesitates, 'worry.'

Shahana wonders what Ayesha almost said but she grabs her hand. 'Come into the forest,' she says, and guides her over the log bridge.

'Do you go out much?' Shahana asks when they are sitting under a chinar tree. All the leaves have dropped; they can see the sky through the branches. Poplars nearby look like straw brooms sweeping the sky.

'Nay, this is the furthest I have been. Of course we go into the garden at night, but Mr Pervaiz brings our food.'

'It has been two years, Ayesha.'

'I know, and I am sorry about your loss also. How are you living?'

Shahana pauses. She realises she can't mention the militant after all. And Zahid? Should she say anything about him yet? Since he has come they have eaten better. Spiced hare has put colour in Tanveer's cheeks. 'Nana-ji taught Tanveer how to fish before he died. And I am embroidering.'

'You? Sewing?'

'Ji, Nana-ji taught me how to do that too.' Then she adds in defence, 'My mother sewed your clothes.'

Ayesha smiles sadly. 'I know. I wish I could still fit into them. Ummie can't sew or do anything anymore.' She stops, as if she has said too much.

'So you are cooking?'

Ayesha nods. 'I do everything.'

'Then we are the same, you and I, except Tanveer gets the firewood and fish. And he is learning to milk Rani.' She stops as she remembers who is teaching him that.

'Ummie is so sad, she doesn't remember how to do normal things. She sits in a dream most of the time.'

'Tell her we need her.'

Ayesha frowns. 'She won't understand.'

'How can we make her better?'

'I don't know.'

'What if I speak to her?' Shahana says.

'She hasn't spoken to anyone in the village since Abu disappeared. Some people say he left to fight with the militants but he wouldn't have deserted us.'

'Maybe the police thought he was going to do that and put him in prison. Even if he is with the militants he would have been forced to fight,' Shahana says, thinking of Zahid and Tanveer. Could Zahid help? His father has disappeared too.

'We just need to know. It is the unknowing that has crippled Ummie.'

They are quiet for a moment, then Shahana says, 'Ayesha?'

'Ji?'

'I think I am in trouble.' Ayesha is a year older; surely she will know how to help.

'What sort of trouble?' Ayesha's frown deepens. 'You need money? We still have some left.'

'No. I embroider for Mr Nadir and he pays me.'

'Nadir Akbar's cloth shop?'

'Ji.' Shahana takes a deep breath. 'And I think he has made me an offer of marriage on behalf of a friend of his.'

'But we come from educated families; we are too young to think of things like this.'

'I know it. I have refused but I don't think he believed me.' Shahana holds Ayesha's hand. 'I am frightened to go back but I have to take my embroidery work to him. What shall I do? I need an adult to speak to him on my behalf.'

'Finish the work and I will take it. I can say you are ill.'

'But you don't go out of the house.'

Ayesha nods. 'If I have to go somewhere like today, I wear this.' She pulls at the burqa.

'But if you go for me the matter won't be settled.'

'It will give you more time.'

'What if he has a proposal for you as well?'

Ayesha smiles. 'I will say my mother has already decided on another. Besides,' her smile fades, 'no one will want a marriage with me until we find out what happened to Abu.'

'Oh, Ayesha.' Shahana hugs her. 'I knew you wouldn't forget our friendship.'

'I never will, but I have to return now.'

'How shall we know to meet?'

'You can bring the sewing to the house. Ummie is used to hearing people come to the door. But to talk together?' She stops to think. 'You can leave a note under the door and I'll come when Ummie is resting.'

—o—o—o—

When Shahana returns Zahid and Tanveer are under the house. Tanveer is showing Zahid how well he can cut up a fish. He is laughing. Zahid looks up as Shahana passes by. She wants to say they were a long time and ask what they were doing, but she has a secret of her own now and doesn't want Zahid to ask about her day.

It is Tanveer who asks. 'What did you do all morning, Shahji?' Then he adds cheekily, 'Did you miss us?'

It is a long time since she has seen him so playful. She smiles at him. 'I stitched and—' She hesitates. 'I spoke to Ayesha at last.'

Tanveer moves his shoulders like a Bollywood dancer. 'What good news. Is Aunty Rabia better?'

Shahana's eyes feel cloudy. 'Nay, but at least Ayesha is speaking.'

Zahid doesn't ask who Ayesha is and Shahana understands something about herself and Zahid: people with a secret don't ask many questions. Tanveer has no secrets and so asks questions all day.

'Did you see anything dangerous by the river?' she asks carefully.

'Militants, you mean?' Tanveer wipes his knife.

Shahana started. 'I mean dogs,' she says in a strangled voice.

Zahid says, 'Only in the distance.'

'There seem to be fewer dogs,' Tanveer adds.

Maybe Shahana should tell them what Mr Pervaiz said about militants so Zahid could be on guard? But Zahid knows there are militants in the area. He saw them himself. Best to keep away from the subject altogether.

Zahid stands. 'Will you give me a potato? Your oldest one. Tanveer and I can plant it.'

'But we will need to eat it.'

'With plants you have to think ahead. Sometimes you have to sacrifice one to have more food when you are in greater need.'

Shahana doesn't think they will have one old enough for planting, but one is softer than the others. When she brings it out, Zahid shows her the white nodules.

'See these? They will grow once put in the ground.'

'Winter is beginning,' Shahana points out.

'Ji, but it will be safe until the snow melts.'

Chapter 11

Shahana was running through the forest, her feet skimming across the leaves that covered the ground. A man with a grey beard was chasing her. He called, 'Stop, I will marry you.'

'Nay!' she cried.

She climbed right up the mountain where the giant fence shadowed the forest. At the top a young man in a white cap stood knee-deep in the snow. It was Irfan.

'Bring me your little brother,' he said, 'and I will help you. You will have no more fear.'

Then his cap changed into a turban and his face flickered until it was Zahid's.

Shahana springs awake. Rani is bleating to be milked under the house. Tanveer is nowhere to be seen, and Shahana wonders where he has gone without Rani. She checks under the house; Zahid has gone too, and yes, they have taken the rifle. She hopes the onions she has left will stretch to another hare curry.

She takes her sewing and sits on the logs outside; it

is too cold now on the ground. She is thinking of Ayesha when she hears a man's voice.

'Assalamu alaikum.'

She looks up and sees it is the militant. He walks very quietly. Maybe they learn how to do that at the militants' camp. She puts her needle through the cloth and stands up. 'Janab?' She forces her face to stay immobile, even though the rest of her shakes like autumn leaves.

He has the empty Sprite bottle in his hand.

'It is only two days,' she says. Then she bites her lip. Will he think she is complaining and be angry?

'I said I wouldn't come every day.'

She has Zahid to feed as well. What if the milk doesn't last? Well, she would go without. She is not sure what the militant will do to her if she refuses. Would he use the gun? She takes the bottle inside and fills it.

When she comes out the man is squatting by Rani and talking to her. 'What is her name?' he asks when Shahana hands him the milk.

'Rani,' she says.

'I am not surprised, she is just like a queen.'

He is not so frightening, squatted by the goat. Rani is nibbling the tail of his turban and he doesn't stop her. 'I have a sister just like you,' he says suddenly.

Shahana looks at him in shock. She thought he was going to say he too has a goat, not a *sister*.

'Her name is Neelum, the same as your river. Every time I look at it I think of her. How brave and proud she is.' Then he stares up at Shahana. 'Like you.'

Shahana blinks. He is a militant. Men like him killed

Irfan and her mother. She doesn't want to hear about his sister.

'She is your age and she likes sewing also.' He glances at the pheran as if he wishes his sister were there, sewing it herself. 'She attends school. Do you?'

His eyes are compelling and she tries not to look at him directly. She knows she has to answer him; he is too strong. Maybe if she answers his questions he will go away, up the mountain back to his camp.

'My tent school was shelled. There is no school here now.'

He stands up and Rani playfully butts his legs. 'Is there no one to teach you?' He reaches out a hand to scratch Rani's head.

'The teacher is unwell. She is a half-widow.'

The young man nods as though he understands, but Shahana is sure he doesn't.

'Many men in my family don't think girls should be educated but I disagree with this view.'

Shahana doesn't want to hear his views either. She looks out in the direction of the river. No one is trudging up the slope. No boys are walking down the mountain. When will he leave? *Chello, move, go, go!* She shouts it in her head.

'Actually, I don't agree about this jihad.'

Shahana swings up her head to stare at him. What did he just say?

'I am a true Muslim and the longer I am with the militants the more I am led to believe jihad is the way to peace, but I thought it would be different. Innocent children are caught in the crossfire. It is not why I joined. I came so Muslim brothers and sisters would have freedom, but we are killing them, destroying their culture, not freeing them.'

Shahana watches him, fascinated. He sounds like a young man who wants to go home.

'What do you think, little sister?'

Shahana opens her mouth, but nothing comes out. He has called her his *sister*. What does that mean to a fighter like him?

'No thoughts?' he prompts, as if disappointed.

No one has asked her what she thinks. Dare she say it?

'I think...' She licks her bottom lip. 'I think there should not be militants or the army here. That the governments should make peace, so children's lives aren't destroyed. There should be no fence dividing us.' She checks his face. Is he angry? What will he do now?

The young man gives a short laugh yet he still doesn't smile at her.

She waits to see what kind of laugh it is.

'I was right about you. Not only brave, but honest as well.' Then he lays his right hand over his heart. Her father used to do that. It takes all of Shahana's self control not to weep. 'I am Amaan Khan. I don't know for how long you will see me, but while I am here you and your brothers will be safe, little sister.' He holds up a five-rupee note to her. It is too much again for the milk but she accepts it. He lifts the milk as if saluting her and then he leaves with Rani bleating after him.

Shahana now knows more about the militant than she knows about Zahid, who lives under her house as her relative. The boys have brought home a water bird; Zahid showed Tanveer how to build a trap to catch it. That night after they have eaten and Tanveer is asleep she ignores her own secret and asks Zahid a personal question. She asks if he has a brother like Tanveer.

He is quiet for so long that she is sorry she asked. People who take a long time to answer are wading through memories, trying to decide how to tell the story. She has picked up her embroidery when Zahid finally speaks.

'I did have a brother. He was throwing stones. The soldiers fired above the crowd of boys, but still a bullet found my brother.' Then he adds quietly, 'I was there. My mother told me to keep him safe.'

He gulps as if his air is gone and Shahana doesn't say a word.

'The soldiers get a bounty when they shoot someone suspected of being a militant. They called my brother a militant and so my father marched.' He is blinking back tears. 'When the van pulled up outside our house they pushed him in the back of it, and we have not seen him since. My mother kept me at home for weeks. I was not allowed outside except to relieve myself in the dark. She said she wouldn't lose us all. That was when she sat in the park with other mothers and wives who had lost husbands and sons.' He sighs. 'Then we moved to the village and one day I did go outside—' He stops again.

'And you came here,' Shahana prompted.

Zahid turns to look at her. She can see the thoughts fighting in his eyes, but all he says is, 'Ji, I came here.'

Shahana tells him about Irfan then. It is the first time she has told this story. When she is finished Zahid's hand is covering hers.

'They should ask us what we think of war,' he says softly.

She remembers her conversation with the militant that morning. 'Ji, I have much to say.'

Zahid picks up the flute and plays a folk song. Tears prick Shahana's eyes as she sews her silver leaves.

Chapter 12

Clouds are hanging low over the house. It is so cold now that Shahana takes out her pheran from the clothes trunk and puts it on. It is grey wool, like most pherans, but she has embroidered flowers and leaves in bright colours around the cuffs and on the front. She picks up Tanveer's pheran and sees Nana-ji's old brown one folded up in the trunk. She has been keeping his pheran for when Tanveer grows, but this winter Zahid will need it.

The boys are outside with Rani when she emerges with the robes. The wind is cold and the boys are making Rani trot between them by offering pieces of stale roti. Rani butts Zahid and Tanveer giggles.

Shahana stands still awhile, staring at Tanveer's happy mouth. Then she calls them. She hands the larger pheran to Zahid. She notices how Tanveer watches as he puts it on.

'Ji, Tanveer,' Shahana says, for she knows what he is

thinking. 'It is Nana-ji's, but if Zahid is careful with it you can still wear it in a few years' time.'

'Shukriya,' Zahid says. 'That feels better. I thought we would have to run races with Rani all day to keep warm.'

'It will get much colder.' Shahana helps Tanveer put his arms through the long sleeves.

Then she brings Nana-ji's scythe from under the house. 'Have you used one of these?' she asks Zahid.

'Zarur, certainly. It is how my mother and I survived in the village – by clearing land and planting vegetables.'

'We will not clear land,' Shahana says. 'We will cut grass for the floor. And we will take Rani to carry it.' Her words are short and sharp today and she's not sure how to fix them. Sometimes it is difficult to see Tanveer so happy with Zahid. How will he feel when Zahid leaves?

She leads them to a secluded part of the little river. She doesn't want to go so close to the river but it is where the best bulrush reeds are. A mist settles low on the water. Tanveer holds Rani's rope and Zahid watches all around them. He has brought the rifle.

'There are no dogs today,' Tanveer says. 'Usually when it's cold the dogs come closer.'

Shahana can't decide if he is pleased or disappointed. She also wonders if Zahid is watching for something else. Militants, perhaps?

Shahana stares in fascination as Zahid takes off his pheran and picks up the scythe to cut the bulrushes. His body is fluid, swishing the scythe against the grass.

It is like watching the river curl along the bank in summer and she is lulled into stillness. Tanveer calls for a turn and Shahana shakes some sense into her head.

'You can collect the grass in bundles.' She says it crossly; this is not the way to be thinking of a brother. She pushes the thoughts of Zahid away.

As Zahid cuts, Shahana and Tanveer tie the grass with the green string and secure it onto Rani's back. When Zahid finishes, she says, 'We will hang this from the rafters and dry it over the fire, and when it's very cold we'll spread it on the floor.' She thinks of Ayesha's house and how they won't need to cut grass – they will have carpets.

The militant doesn't come that week. Shahana finishes embroidering the pheran with the silver thread. She uses a little silver thread to add a star in a small piece of embroidery of her own that she is doing. She prepares a square for Tanveer to sew as well. Maybe he will become as skilful as Nana-ji and they can sell small pieces that can be sewn into the front of shirts, like a bodice. It is hard to find time to embroider; there is so much to do to prepare for the winter: collecting extra wood, drying the hare flesh that Zahid is providing, hanging the grass to dry next to the apricots drying from summer.

Once they have finished hanging the grass bundles, Shahana decides to take the embroidered pheran to Ayesha. She leaves the boys stacking firewood under the house. Zahid has the axe and is chopping smaller pieces for kindling.

She sighs heavily as she crosses the log bridge. What

will Mr Nadir say when Ayesha returns the pheran? Maybe she should go herself. Maybe Ayesha will be in danger. But is Shahana in danger herself? Has she imagined it? She's had a proposal, and she has refused, that is all. So why does she feel so trapped?

Shahana stands outside Ayesha's door. Should she leave it on the step? She calls out once. 'Ayesha.' As she bends to put the pheran down, the door opens.

'Chup,' Ayesha whispers. 'Today you can come in. Ummie is resting but we can sit in the other room.'

Shahana follows Ayesha through the door. She remembers this big room. Aunty Rabia is sitting in a chair dozing in front of the TV. There is no sound, just the light from the TV flickering.

'Even though she doesn't go out, she likes to see the news,' Ayesha says softly. 'I think she is hoping for some word of Abu. But it won't happen.'

In the other room there is a desk with a laptop computer on it.

'You have a computer,' Shahana says with wonder.

'It was— I mean, it is Abu's.' She corrects herself and there is a short silence. Shahana thinks how difficult it must be not to know whether to say 'was' or 'is'.

'He did all his business on it,' Ayesha continues. 'Every now and then people email us for a carpet. We give shop owners a commission to handle the sale. It is just enough for our living.'

'If your mother doesn't go to the bazaar—' Shahana stops, not sure how to form the words without being disrespectful.

'I am running my father's business. I give the carpet information to Mr Nadir,' Ayesha says.

Mr Nadir? Shahana is disturbed by his name. 'So you have dealings with him too?'

'Only by email. Of course I can only do it when the electricity is working.'

Ayesha shows Shahana the computer. 'Sometimes there is low shedding or no connection. It is very difficult through the winter – the dish doesn't work as well then.'

She opens a page on the computer and Shahana stares at it.

'See this? This is an email. It's like a letter but it arrives immediately – no waiting for old Baba-ji to bring the mail. I don't have to meet anyone I send an email to.'

Shahana doesn't relax. Mr Nadir reminds her of a spider with a sticky web catching flies. She doesn't want to be one of those flies, nor does she want Ayesha to be. 'You must be careful,' she murmurs.

She fingers the keys. If her mother was alive she would have a computer like this. Both she and Aunty Rabia taught in the school. There was a desktop computer in Shahana's home once.

'I want to show you something,' Ayesha says. She presses some keys. It takes a long time for the page to show on the screen. When it does, Shahana sees it is a site for children about peace. It is written in both Urdu and Angrezi. There are children's stories written on the page, and pictures painted by children.

Tears well up in Shahana's eyes.

'And look,' Ayesha says. 'Here is a page about what children can do. They are meeting with a minister from the government after the winter. He will come to the Neelum Valley and hear children's stories and see their artwork.'

'What good can it do?' Shahana bursts out.

Ayesha doesn't speak straight away. Then she says, 'Surely it is good to tell our stories?'

'It might be too late,' Shahana says in a small voice.

Ayesha puts an arm around Shahana's shoulders. 'We can prepare stories together and send them to the website.'

Shahana looks at her, amazed. 'You know how to do that?'

Ayesha dips her head to show she does. 'And soon you will too. We always tell stories through the winter,' she says. 'Didn't your grandfather tell stories?'

Shahana nods. This winter would be bleak indeed without Nana-ji telling his stories. Maybe they were even the ones he had told her mother when she was young.

'Shahana.' Ayesha holds her hand. 'This winter you have to tell the stories.'

That is when Shahana cries. 'I am so tired of being the one to keep Tanveer safe, the one to worry, the one to tell stories. I want someone to tell me stories.'

It is the first time Shahana has wept this hard since her father died. She didn't dare cry like this when Nana-ji died; she didn't want to upset Tanveer.

Ayesha puts her head close to Shahana's and gently

says, 'Aram se, be calm,' but Shahana cannot stop. She cries for Tanveer, for herself because of Mr Nadir, and out of fear. What if the militant steals Tanveer, or if someone finds out about Zahid? She will be worse than a half-widow. She hiccups. At least no one will want to marry her then. But could something more terrible happen?

Chapter 13

It is cold but Shahana has much to be thankful for. The militant hasn't come for another week, she is friends with Ayesha again, and the last time she went to their house Aunty Rabia actually looked at her as if she remembered her. Tanveer catches a trout in the river and that night, full of fish and yoghurt, Shahana tells a story.

It is one of Nana-ji's stories, about a king who had two sons. She can tell by Tanveer's smile that he remembers it.

'The king's first wife died on the birthing bed having twin boys,' she starts, 'and much later the king married again. The boys were as old as Zahid by then and the new wife was young. She thought the boys were handsome and she wanted to kiss them. They refused and said, "You are our stepmother."'

'And she got so angry,' Tanveer says, 'that she told lies about them and ordered them to be killed.'

'Ji,' Shahana carries on, 'but the huntsman who took them into the forest to kill them let them go and they fled to the next kingdom where they became bodyguards to that king.

'One night, in the neighbouring kingdom, there was a snake sliding up the king and queen's bed. One of the princes, now a bodyguard, killed it. His bloody sword was raised in his hand when the king suddenly woke. The king thought he and his wife were being murdered. He shouted for the palace guard and ordered the prince to be put in prison. The prince's brother was serving in the palace guard and said, "Sire, isn't it best to inquire first and punish later?" He walked around the bed and found the dead snake. "Would your bodyguard have been killing this serpent and not you?"'

'Yes,' Tanveer adds with glee. 'After that, the king always asked questions before he punished people. And there were two princesses that the brothers married as well.'

Shahana isn't sure she has told the story correctly. There were other parts of it that Nana-ji said, which made it last a lot longer, but Tanveer is happy, and right then that is all that matters to Shahana.

Tanveer tells a story of his own. Zahid looks amused as he starts.

'This is about a prince too. He became lost in the forest and everyone thought he was dead. And then one day his younger sister and brother found a big boy just like him. They rescued him from the wolves and discovered that he was their long lost brother returned. He had come back to protect the kingdom through the freezing winter.'

There is a long silence. Shahana glances at Zahid in dismay, then back to Tanveer. Does he truly believe Zahid is their brother? Surely not. Finally, she says to him, 'That is a good story.' But she sees the intense look he bestows on Zahid, and again Shahana is afraid.

'I have a story also,' Zahid says then. His story is a funny one, about a haunted mosque and how a clever boy rids the mosque of evil jinns.

Tanveer laughs and Shahana relaxes. Tanveer can be sensitive for all his brightness and questions. She'll never forget how the night before Nana-ji died, Tanveer said, 'He will not leave us alone.' After Nana-ji died the next day, Tanveer didn't speak for weeks. Shahana tried to explain how people cannot choose their time to die, but he wouldn't listen. It wasn't until he found her crying by Rani that he spoke. Rani had just kicked her bucket. Shahana felt Tanveer's small arm sneak around her neck. 'Shahji?' he said.

⌐o─o─o⌐

The next day Shahana takes Tanveer with her to Ayesha's. He has been asking to see Aunty Rabia, and besides, all his questions may help Aunty Rabia to remember things. Ayesha sits Tanveer next to Aunty Rabia on the couch and gives him his embroidery to do. The TV flickers off and Shahana sees Tanveer's hand sneak across to touch Aunty Rabia's before he starts stitching. She doesn't say anything but she looks content.

'Is she getting better?' Shahana asks Ayesha in the next room.

Ayesha quotes an old proverb. '*Drop by drop the river fills*. She's better than before. Having you come has helped and it is slicing through the sorrow. She is taking an interest again.' Shaking her head in amazement, she lights a lamp. 'Sorry, the bijily, the electricity, has just gone off.'

Shahana thinks how it is always off at her own house.

Ayesha reaches across to a paper bag on the bed. It is the sort of bag Mr Nadir uses and Shahana feels as if she's swallowed stones.

'I told Mr Nadir that you were sick and I was bringing your work. He liked it very much and he gave me another garment for you to embroider. Here it is.'

Shahana doesn't take it. 'I was hoping he'd be annoyed with me for not coming and that would be the end of it.'

Ayesha frowns. 'Men like Mr Nadir do not let go of a pot of gold. He was about to pay you some measly sum so I asked for more. He gave it willingly. He knows what your work is worth, Shahana, so don't accept less than this.' She hands Shahana thirty rupees.

'But that's more than double.'

'It is silver work on wool. And you are an artist. He as good as said so.'

'I can buy Tanveer's medicine now.' Shahana presses her lips together. She didn't mean to say that aloud.

Ayesha seems not to have heard but after a while she

says, as if it is unrelated, 'If you ever need anything like medicine, come and ask us. It would be our honour to help in any way.'

Shahana smiles. It is what her father would have said. How strange that both Ayesha and herself do men's work and talk like men now.

'What is in the bag? Mr Nadir looked very satisfied with himself when he gave it to me.'

Shahana opens it and takes out a dupatta. But not any dupatta: it is the scarf of a princess or a bride. It is red and the spool of thread he has included is gold.

'Gold,' Ayesha whispers. 'Pure gold. He told me you are not to waste any or use more than you should.'

'He says that every time.' Shahana can't touch the dupatta, nor feel any excitement over using gold thread. He has sent her a message. For all she knows this may be her very own wedding dupatta. She drops it back into the bag and looks out the window. The wind is rising, and dark clouds scud across the sky.

'A storm is coming. We must go. Can I leave the dupatta here in case I get it wet on the way home?'

'Certainly. And here, I have something for Tanveer. I have grown out of these now.' She holds out a coat, plastic shoes and woollen socks.

'Thank you. He will like them very much.'

Shahana stands up. They haven't worked on their stories for the website, but she is nervous about the weather. When they tell Tanveer it is time to go he leans over and kisses Aunty Rabia on the cheek, and something remarkable happens. She smiles at him. It is as if it is two years ago and they have visited like they used to.

Ayesha catches her breath loudly. 'It was good of you to bring Tanveer,' she says. 'He is a noble boy.'

Shahana blinks. Ayesha has spoken truly. All the care that Shahana has given Tanveer has been worth it. Maybe Tanveer's ease with people is because he has suffered himself. She puts the coat on him over his pheran and the plastic shoes on his feet.

Tanveer smiles his thanks at Ayesha. 'Can I come again?' he says.

'Our door is open to you,' Ayesha says. 'Our house is your house.'

This makes Shahana smile; it is what Nana-ji said when they went to live with him.

As they walk down the steps to the road, Shahana marvels at how quickly the weather can change. The rain is only just starting as they reach the log bridge, but Shahana knows the rain will turn to snow when the air freezes. 'Come,' she says to Tanveer, 'we must hurry.' She holds out her hand, for the icy logs are like walking on slippery glass, but he skips ahead.

'I will race you home.' He turns as he says it and that is when he slips.

'Tanveer!' She is too far away. She lunges for him but just catches his coat. It slips out of her fingers, and she falls to her knees as the stream carries him away. She runs off the bridge along the bank. What can she do? She can't swim. She screams his name over and over. She can't lose him too. She races along the stream, straining to outrun the water. If she could just get ahead of him, throw in a stick...

But someone is already there. A boy plunges into the water and grabs Tanveer. They are both swept away but the other boy is gradually heading for the bank.

Shahana runs down to help pull them out. It is Zahid. He protects Tanveer by some rocks where they can't be washed away again but he doesn't pull Tanveer up the bank.

'Take him,' is all he says. It is as if they are the only words he has.

Shahana climbs down and lifts Tanveer. She doesn't know where the strength comes from. Then Zahid drags himself up to the top of the bank and lies still for some moments in the mud, gasping. Shahana can only think of Tanveer. His eyes are closed.

Zahid pulls himself to his knees and presses on Tanveer's chest. 'Turn him on his side.'

Tanveer curls up and coughs. Water dribbles out of his mouth.

'Come.' Shahana picks up Tanveer. She is soaked from the rain and Tanveer's wet clothes. 'We have to carry him home.'

Chapter 14

Tanveer's lungs are weak, Shahana knows this, and a dunking in the stream is the last thing he needs. Zahid drags his feet but he helps lift Tanveer up the logs to the house. Shahana lights the fire while Zahid starts pulling off Tanveer's clothes. Shahana finds dry clothes for Tanveer and some of Nana-ji's clothes for Zahid. She dries Tanveer and dresses him, then turns her head as Zahid takes off his clothes.

Shahana lays Tanveer on the charpoy. He is breathing but he hasn't opened his eyes. She wishes he was already grown. Apparently Nana-ji had weak lungs when he was young and he grew to be an old man of almost sixty before he died last winter.

'You are wet too,' Zahid reminds her. 'I'll sit with him while you change.'

Shahana can see the sense of this. If she should get cold and sick what would happen to Tanveer? Zahid turns his back and murmurs to Tanveer.

Shahana has looked after Tanveer since he was tiny.

She knows all about boys' bodies but she is ashamed now to be changing in the same room as Zahid. She peels off her clothes in stages as she usually does, dries herself and puts on a clean shalwar and qameez. She hangs the pherans and wet clothes to dry on hooks in the rafters. Then she makes chai in the samovar and they drink it watching Tanveer.

'He slipped,' she says. 'We were hurrying to get home before the storm.'

Zahid nods and Shahana is glad he doesn't speak, for she has no energy to listen. She puts a blanket over Tanveer and hopes he is just sleeping. She glances at Zahid and sees how exhausted he is. How did he survive in the big river when he is so spent from being in the stream for a few minutes? The thought leaves her as Tanveer stirs.

He opens his eyes. 'Shahji?'

The tears come suddenly. Shahana tries to blink them away. What would she do if something happened to Tanveer? He is the future of their family. She will have failed her parents, Nana-ji and Irfan if she lets anything happen to him. She scoops him up into her arms and hugs him tight. Then he coughs. It racks his whole body and she can hear the whispering in his lungs. She races to the trunk for his medicine.

'Here.' She sits Tanveer up and puts the tablet on his tongue. She gives him some water and watches him swallow, for she knows he doesn't like to take them.

'I'll be fine,' he says, his voice just a croak.

Zahid stares at Tanveer. 'My cousin breathed like

that all the time when she was young. She had a spray medicine that flew straight to her lungs.'

Shahana nods. 'We have that too but I try the tablets first. If he is worse in the night we will use the spray.'

In the night Tanveer wakes crying. He can't breathe. Shahana has the spray medicine ready. Every few hours Shahana and Zahid have to use the medicine. Shahana knows it will soon be gone. It is why she tries the tablets first – the spray is so expensive.

By early morning it seems Tanveer is breathing easier.

Shahana turns to Zahid. His eyes are half shut. 'Zahid? Thank you for what you did.'

'He is my brother too.'

Zahid is quiet, so Shahana asks him about his cousin.

He thinks for a moment, then he says softly, 'Her name was Nissa.'

Shahana hears the way he says it, with a sigh on her name, and wishes she hasn't asked, but Zahid keeps talking. 'The soldiers came to her house. She had grown beautiful, my mother said. But soldiers don't care who is beautiful or who is promised in marriage, they take what they want.' His fingers clench onto the spray puffer he is holding for Tanveer and Shahana hopes he doesn't break it.

'She didn't survive?' Shahana says it gently, for she knows that this girl was promised to him.

It is as if he doesn't hear her. 'Soldiers want to keep people frightened. They hurt some to keep the others obedient. I wish the army would leave. There are too many soldiers – they are like locusts eating up our valley.'

'I am sorry.' Shahana whispers it, and she gently brushes the hair from Zahid's eyes with her fingers. He lies down on the floor – he is too weak to sleep under the house while it is snowing. Shahana lies on the charpoy by Tanveer. Outside, the wind tugs at the thatch and wood shingles on the roof. The snow thrashes against the walls. She pulls the quilt up over herself and Tanveer.

Shahana wandered into a beautiful rose garden. Water cascaded into a long pool. She had on a long red and gold skirt and over it a long-sleeved kurta to match. On her head was the wedding dupatta that she had embroidered herself with golden thread. She could hear the wedding band with drums and horns playing for her. She was about to see her bridegroom for the first time. He sat in the tent on a couch and there was room for her. His hair was dark, his eyes grey. He stood tall to help her to the couch. Just as she looked up and saw that it was Zahid, his face changed. She stumbled and suddenly it was Mr Nadir reaching for her. 'What do boys know?' he said. 'I will make you a better husband. You will never have to worry and you will never be cold again.'

Chapter 15

Shahana wakes in the morning and tries to dismiss her nightmares. She would like to sleep without having bad dreams or waking up worrying about Tanveer.

After a week his breathing no longer wakes him at night, although it is harder to rouse him in the mornings. There is snow on the ground all the time now, and the clouds lie low, like a canopy of white cloth hiding the mountains. On mornings when it is not snowing the boys collect more wood and stack it under the house. Shahana does more embroidery squares in the afternoons and Tanveer joins her. If the militant comes again she will ask if he wants to buy one. She never thought she would hope for the militant to return. Now she wonders where he is. She tries to think of him as Amaan – it is a beautiful name meaning faith. Was he faithful? Could she trust him?

One early morning Shahana is sewing in her open doorway to catch the sun as it comes over the mountains when Ayesha appears around the side of the house. It is the first time Ayesha has come to the house. She is wearing the black burqa. At first Shahana is so shocked to see her there she is not sure what to say, and then she remembers Zahid has gone trapping.

'Salaam, Ayesha,' Shahana manages.

Ayesha giggles. 'You look like you've seen a jinn.'

'It is just I wasn't expecting you to come here.'

Ayesha's face becomes serious. 'I need you to visit my home. Ummie is asking for you.'

'For me?'

Ayesha nods. 'Can you come straight away? Sometimes she forgets but she is getting better. This is the first time she has asked something like this.'

'Come inside. Would you like chai?'

Ayesha walks up to the open door. 'Normally I would but we are such good friends, can I refuse this time on account of Ummie?' Then she sees Tanveer still asleep on the charpoy. 'Should we wake him?'

'I'd rather not,' Shahana says. 'He needs to rest. We won't be long, will we?'

Ayesha shakes her head. 'Ummie just wants to talk to you.'

Shahana puts her shawl over her pheran, and slips out the door with Ayesha.

―o―o―o―

Inside Ayesha's house, Aunty Rabia is out of her chair and walking around the room. As soon as she sees Shahana, she invites her to sit on the couch with her while Ayesha makes chai.

'How are you, my child?' Aunty Rabia asks.

'Teik hai, I'm fine, thank you, Aunty-ji.'

Aunty Rabia is looking at her closely. After seeing her in her own private world, facing the TV but not watching it, it is unnerving to see her so focused.

'It is good you are so well, Aunty-ji.' Shahana truly means it. How she has longed for Aunty Rabia to be the family friend that she used to be: her mother's best friend.

'I worry about you and Tanveer up in your grandfather's hut.'

'We are fine.' What could she say? Ayesha might understand, but she couldn't let Aunty Rabia find out about Zahid, or the militant.

'I could come to visit you and see what you need.' Aunty Rabia hesitates. 'I haven't been out of the house yet, but when I am able.'

'You will be very welcome,' Shahana murmurs the polite words but really she is wondering how to graciously decline. Maybe Aunty Rabia will forget about it. She isn't totally well yet. Shahana doesn't even feel she can mention Mr Nadir; what could Aunty Rabia do?

Ayesha brings the chai in then. 'I wish you lived with me,' she says.

Shahana doesn't know what to say. After Nana-ji died she may have wanted that to happen, but how could she now? She has Rani to look after, and Zahid. Her mother's voice tells her Zahid could live by himself, but she doesn't listen. Is it because she likes to pretend she has a big brother again? She doesn't dare think of him as anything else. She shakes her head and her tea spills.

'Are you all right?' Ayesha asks as she uses a tea towel to mop up the mess.

'I'm fine, truly. Your mother is kind to think about us, but we will be fine.' She is thinking of Tanveer then; what if he wakes and finds she's not there? She should have brought him with her. She tries to drink the chai faster but it is too hot.

Shahana hopes Ayesha will not be offended. 'I'm sorry, I need to go. Tanveer may wake up. He might need his medicine.'

'Teik hai, fine.' Ayesha hands her Mr Nadir's paper bag. 'It's not snowing today.'

She takes the bag and Aunty Rabia catches hold of her arm as she stands. 'Remember what I said.'

Shahana nods and thanks her, but as she hurries down to the road, she berates herself. What is she thinking, wanting help from Aunty Rabia, when there is Zahid to explain?

--o--o--o--

When she returns Tanveer is awake. 'A man came, Shahji.'

Shahana stands frozen in the doorway. 'Who?' But she knows what he will say.

'He said he knew you, Shahana. He wanted milk so I gave him some and he gave me ten rupees.' He hands

95

it to her. Why did he give so much? Yet they need it. She puts it in the pocket of her qameez.

There is a mist in Shahana's head. Her heart is beating like wild dogs are fighting in there. How can she ask Tanveer not to tell Zahid about seeing the militant?

All afternoon she worries, starts to tell Tanveer, then stops. It will make it worse – he'll ask Zahid why Shahana didn't want him to know. Her fears are realised when they are eating their evening meal. They have hardly eaten a few bites when Tanveer tells Zahid a man came to the house asking for milk.

Zahid fires questions at him. 'Did you know him? Did he have a weapon? What did he look like?'

Zahid's questions bring the image of Amaan to life as if he were standing there before them.

'So he is a militant.'

'He was nice,' Tanveer ventures.

'What else did he say?' Zahid drops his roti and doesn't bother picking it up.

Tanveer is almost in tears. 'He just asked for milk and said to say salaam to my brother and sister.'

There is a heavy silence while Shahana stares at her plate. Then Zahid turns on her. 'You know this man? How does he know Tanveer has a sister or a brother? Did you say so?' He turns back to Tanveer without leaving her any room to answer. 'Don't you know those men are dangerous? They have such strict ideas. Didn't you see he was a militant?'

He glances at Shahana again. 'You should have told me, warned me.'

Shahana wishes she could explain. She was protecting the boys by giving milk. But she knew all along Zahid would not understand.

'I'm sorry,' is all she says.

'They take boys to fight.'

'He didn't take me,' Tanveer says. 'He smiled at me.'

They stare at him. Shahana wonders what that smile must have looked like, a smile she will never see. Amaan is strong and has piercing eyes but to Shahana he also looks like someone's big brother. Now when she thinks of him she doesn't think of militants killing Irfan.

'Perhaps he will protect us,' she says.

Zahid groans. Whether in frustration or pain, Shahana cannot tell. He pulls her around to face him. The suddenness of his hands on her shoulders shocks her into stillness.

'Shahana, we are a family.'

She gives a wary nod and he lets his hands drop.

'You have to tell me everything that happens. It is dangerous here in the forest. You and Tanveer should live somewhere else.'

Ayesha has said it too, but she would miss Zahid. There, she can admit it now. 'How can we live anywhere else?'

Zahid doesn't answer that. Instead he says, 'Don't forget what they did to your family.'

'They were different ones,' Shahana murmurs.

'All militants are like soldiers. They say they fight for something noble, for freedom, but their methods are the same. The results are the same. People still die.'

She rests her head on her hand. How long will she have to remember what militants and soldiers did? The bitterness of the memory always hurts. She wishes she could let it go, be happy again, but Zahid's words make her feel ashamed.

She remembers Amaan calling her his little sister. 'His name is Amaan,' she says.

At her words, Zahid strides outside to stand on the logs like a sentinel. He has the rifle.

Chapter 16

Shahana and Tanveer are watching Zahid build up the wall under the house to make it warmer. The wind is chilling, and Shahana pulls her shawl closer around her.

'It is too cold down here,' Tanveer protests. He glances at Shahana for confirmation.

Shahana stays silent.

'It is not safe for you,' Zahid answers, but he is watching Shahana. 'If the militant sees me here, he will know I am not your brother.' He pauses. 'But if he knows I am sleeping under the house, it will be better for you.'

Shahana knows he speaks truly. Her mother would have said it too. But still she wonders how he knows what the militant will think.

'How could he know?' she asks. 'You even look like our brother Irfan.'

Zahid hesitates as if he is about to say a difficult thing. 'Shahana…' he starts, but it is all he says. He reaches for the axe. 'Veer and I will collect fir branches for the wall.'

Shahana watches them trudge off, taking Rani with

them, shaking her head and ringing her bell. Shahana stays there in the space under the house where Nana-ji kept his tools and wood for the fire. It was never meant to be lived in. Once the snow grows deeper it will be bitterly cold. Zahid will have to light a fire. Will that be safe under the house?

'Shahana?'

She swings around at the sound of her name. It is Ayesha. 'You startled me.'

Ayesha's mouth is stretched tight; she doesn't even give a greeting. 'Who was that with Tanveer?'

Shahana realises it is not the time to lie. 'His name is Zahid.' She takes Ayesha's hands in her own. 'He is like a brother, like Irfan.'

'Oh, Shahana. I came to see if you are all right. You went so quickly yesterday, and Ummie wondered why you didn't talk about Mr Nadir.'

'You told her about that?'

'Yes, you need help.' She purses her lips. 'But I see your life is even more complicated than you said.'

Shahana sighs. 'Come inside and I will tell you over chai.'

When they have their hands wrapped around cups of salty noon chai, keeping their fingers warm, Shahana speaks again.

'We found him, Tanveer and I, saved him from the wild dogs. He hunts for us. Tanveer loves him. I've never seen him so happy. How could I turn Zahid away?'

'Couldn't you have told the police?'

'Go to Athmuqam? It's too far away, how could I

do that? Besides, they'd put him in the camp or prison. They'd think he was a refugee, a fugitive or a boy militant.'

'And he is none of these things?' Ayesha's voice is sharp.

Shahana hangs her head miserably. 'I don't know.'

'All the more reason why you should live with us.'

'What about Tanveer?'

'He can come too.'

'You are so kind. I will think about it carefully.'

'There is really only one decision to make, Shahana.' Ayesha puts her empty cup on the floor.

'Some more chai?' Shahana lifts the samovar.

At first Ayesha says no, but Shahana asks again. The third time she asks Ayesha sighs and says yes.

'Do you remember those afternoon teas at our house after school? Always three times we had to ask if you wanted more chai and on the third time your mother would say yes.'

'It is the proper way.' Ayesha has not lost her frown. 'So many things are not done properly anymore. It's because of the conflict.' She regards Shahana. 'But not everything has changed – we mustn't forget what is haram. Do you know what could happen if someone from the village sees this boy here?'

'Zahid, his name is Zahid,' Shahana says softly, and Ayesha stares at her.

'You could be put into prison for adultery.'

'But I have never—'

'No, but mud will stick, worse than that thrown at a

101

half-widow. Everyone knows there is no mud without rain.'

Shahana nods miserably, trying to push away the image of the three of them sleeping inside the house for warmth. When she is with Zahid she wishes she could forget the rules.

—o—o—o—

That night she thinks about it. She knows it is cold for Zahid under the house and it will get worse. If she goes to Ayesha's then Zahid could sleep in the house. Isn't living at Ayesha's what she secretly wished for before they were speaking again? But that was before she and Tanveer found Zahid. She drifts into sleep and a voice like Nana-ji's reminds her that Zahid is only there to keep them safe. Once she goes to live with Ayesha he will leave.

—o—o—o—

She danced into the forest. It was aflame with autumn leaves, but then right before her eyes they turned into true flames. The flames jumped from tree to tree. The branches were alight – the forest was on fire. Myna birds flew above her. Blue mountain sheep, leopards, hares, wild goats, black panthers and bears thundered through the trees towards the giant fence, but they couldn't jump over it. There was nothing she could do. The animals roared and wailed and squealed. Rani! She had to save Rani from the fire. She ran back towards the house. Just as she reached the logs she heard a gun fire.

102

Shahana springs awake. Gunshots always wake her. Was it in the dream or in the forest? It was so loud. How close was it? She can hear banging. It sounds as if it is coming from under the house.

Tanveer wakes then. 'Shahji?'

She holds him. Rani is bleating.

'Maybe it's the militant. Maybe he wants us for fighters. Maybe he wants Rani.'

'Chup.' Shahana shushes him. 'He wouldn't do that.' But she isn't sure.

She wants to go to the door to check, but she must keep Tanveer safe. Then they hear a snarl. A growl. Rani squeals. Shahana has never heard such a sound. Another gunshot. Is it Zahid?

'Shahji, we have to help Rani.' Tanveer is crying but he jumps off the charpoy and runs to the door.

'Tanveer, stop. Let me light the lamp.'

Suddenly all is quiet. Tanveer peeks out the doorway. 'There's a chitta, Shahji. It's running away.'

She sees the leopard streaking through the trees like silver in the moonlight. 'Get away from the door, Tanveer.'

'But I can hear Rani crying.'

The bleating comes closer, accompanied by click-clacking up the logs. There is a bang on the door and Tanveer opens it wider. 'Zahid.'

Shahana goes to him. 'Are you all right? We didn't know what was happening.'

He leads Rani inside. She is thrashing her head from side to side and complaining pitifully.

'Just a chitta.' He gestures to Rani. 'She will have to sleep in here. The wall didn't hold against a chitta. And Rani on a rope is easy food.'

'I wish I saw the chitta up close,' Tanveer says.

'I saw enough for both of us. She was beautiful but very hungry.'

'You're not hurt?' Shahana says, shutting the door against the cold.

'No, but Rani has a scratch.'

Rani's scratch is a gash across her thigh. Shahana washes it and applies salt, her stock treatment for wounds. There were times Nana-ji brought Rani inside too. She wonders how he knew when to.

Tanveer finds a plastic bag and ties it around Rani's rump. 'This way we can catch her poo.' He ties Rani to the post holding up the roof.

'It will be crowded in here,' Shahana murmurs.

'But warmer,' Zahid grins. 'We can think what else to do tomorrow.'

'Tomorrow we'll make a pen for her,' Shahana says with some satisfaction. She won't be able to leave the house yet, not until Rani is settled.

Chapter 17

In the morning Tanveer finishes sweeping snow off the logs and runs down to play with Rani. He still looks pale, and his shoulders are hunched in his pheran, but he sounds happy. Shahana helps Zahid nail a spare blanket above the door to keep the cold out, then they build the goat pen in the room.

'By the door would be best.' She hasn't slept well. Rani took a long time to settle, and Shahana is still worrying about Ayesha's words. If she tells Zahid about Ayesha's offer he will tell her to go. But will he stay?

'We need to use hard wood or Rani will eat her way through it, and butt you awake in the night.' Zahid is making a joke, and Shahana is glad there doesn't seem to be a barrier between them today. Maybe the leopard attack has made them see what is more important.

Zahid is resting a piece of wood on another, getting ready to nail it with Nana-ji's hammer, when a man's voice echoes from outside.

'Assalamu alaikum.'

They hear Tanveer's voice in reply. 'Wa alaikum assalam. Do you want some milk?'

'Nahin, not today.'

Shahana stands like stone and Zahid carefully lays down the hammer. 'I have to go out there,' she whispers. She puts her shawl over her head.

'Be careful.' Zahid touches her shoulder.

'He won't hurt us,' she says. 'Stay here.'

Shahana can hear Tanveer chatting; she steps through the doorway and nods to Amaan.

When he sees her, he says, 'I was worried. I heard shots from this direction in the night. Are you all right?'

'Ji hahn, yes, thank you.'

'Are all of you okay?'

Shahana nods. Surely he isn't going to ask where her other brother is.

'Tanveer says you had a chitta.'

'Ji, our brother fired shots in the air and it fled.'

'And your goat?' Rani has already nudged against him; he is eyeing her flank.

Shahana gives a flicker of a smile. 'She is fine. We will bring her inside for the winter now.'

There is a slight pause, then the militant says evenly, 'How do you have a weapon?'

Shahana clutches her shawl to her chest to still the jumping of her heart. She breathes deeply before she speaks. 'It is our grandfather's. He died last winter.'

The militant frowns. 'I do not like it that you kids are here alone, even if you do have an older brother. Can you not live with someone in the village?'

'I will think about that, thank you. I have friends in the village.' Shahana realises what she has said and feels unexpected joy well up. She does have friends; they are not alone.

'Shukriya,' she says to him as if he is the one who has brought her friends. She takes a square of embroidery from her pocket. 'I made this for you, for your sister,' she says. It is the piece with the silver star sewn with forbidden thread.

He looks at it then says, 'This is exceptional work. You have great talent.' He brings out some money and Shahana takes a step backwards.

'Nay, janab. It is a gift.'

But he says, 'So is this. Let an honorary brother give you something to ease your circumstances.' He passes it to Tanveer.

'Shukriya, Amaan,' he says.

She feels prickling behind her eyes. When has Tanveer learned to use his name so easily?

Amaan is looking right into her face, his eyes glistening. Then he smiles at Tanveer. When he looks up at her again, the smile is politely erased but she can see it brimming in his eyes.

'Thank you,' she whispers. Tanveer hands her the money, but she is thanking Amaan for the smile.

When she returns Zahid is pacing.

'Did you see him?' she asks, for the door is ajar.

Zahid nods. 'A man like that will know—'

Shahana cuts him off. 'You always say that but you never explain.'

107

Zahid glances at her, as if deciding, then says, 'He was one of the militants who saw Veer and me on the mountain.'

'So? We can't know what he is thinking just because he is a militant. He is different – he misses his family. That's why he comes.'

Zahid hesitates, as though he wants to disagree, but doesn't say any more.

Tanveer rushes up the logs. 'Shahji, I will take Rani and collect some more wood. Maybe I'll see the chitta.'

Zahid is still finishing the pen. Shahana says, 'Don't be long. You are still getting better.' She goes to the door. 'It looks like a snowstorm will come later.'

'Don't worry so much, Shahji. I'm not a baby. I'm big enough now to look after you.'

His words silence Shahana. She feels like warning him to be careful, but she stops herself. Does she treat him like a baby just because he is often unwell? She watches him from the doorway, tying the baskets on Rani and clicking his tongue to make her follow him, 'Tsk, tsk.' Just like Nana-ji.

She returns inside, sits on the charpoy and opens the bag with the dupatta inside. If she embroiders it will it mean she agrees to be married? Could she send it back undone? No, she needs the money. Maybe she can sew it and take it to him to say she won't be the one wearing it. Could she be as brave as a leopard? She smiles at the image of herself snarling at Mr Nadir but her amusement soon fades. If she ever had any courage, it has been sucked from her, like juice from an apple.

The gold thread is on a spool, just like the silver. She threads a needle and tries a few stitches. It is not as fine as cotton or silk, but it shines like silver. The silver thread looked like moonlight on snow. This gold is like sunlight shining on flames. Shahana knows the sun is made of fire; her mother told her so. She loves the sun but she won't see much of it now. Not for the first time, she wonders if they will survive the winter. That makes her think of Ayesha. There is no reason this year not to survive. She just has to decide to stay with Ayesha.

Zahid puts the last length of branch on the pen and disappears outside. He is edgy. Shahana can see that the militants bother him. If she takes Tanveer and goes to Ayesha's, Zahid can stay in the house. If he leaves or can't look after Rani, maybe Shahana can take her to Ayesha's, too, though Rani won't be able to stay inside at Aunty Rabia's.

She is halfway around the border of the dupatta when she looks up. The sky is so dark already it is difficult to see her stitches. She can hear Zahid under the house. Is he trying to fix the damage done by the leopard? She goes down to see.

Zahid has made some mud bricks. 'It's not the right weather to make these, but maybe they will dry. Then we can stack them on this side.'

Shahana doesn't think they will hold a leopard. She says so.

'It's just to keep warmer,' Zahid says. 'The chitta shouldn't come if Rani is inside with you.'

'But what about you? Won't the chitta smell you?'

Zahid stares at her. 'Chittas are not known for eating boys, only goats.'

Then Shahana says quickly before she changes her mind, 'I could take Tanveer and stay at Aunty Rabia's house. She is getting better. Then you will be safer. You can live inside.'

'That will be good for you,' Zahid says slowly. 'Veer...' and he stops.

She knows what he is thinking. Tanveer will not want to leave him. But she can't ask Zahid to look after Tanveer. He often needs medicine, and she sometimes wakes in the night to see to him. And where would Zahid get the money to buy rice and tea? And what if he can't cook? No, she can't leave Tanveer.

She worries afresh that if she goes, Zahid will live somewhere else, somewhere the militant won't come. But before he can say anything else they hear voices.

'Quick, in here!' Zahid gestures to the other side of the wall he is fixing with branches and mud.

'But it might be someone I know,' Shahana says.

'Just in case.'

They crouch together but Shahana can't hear what the voices are saying. A small group of men in turbans pass by near the spring. She can't see if they have guns. None of them look like Amaan.

'See? Your militant has told them where you live. That you have two brothers.' Zahid says the words quietly, but they sting like a scorpion strike.

Surely Amaan would not have done that. He could

have taken Tanveer anytime, but he hasn't. The men move away up the mountain.

Shahana stands and moves out from under the house. She checks the sky. It's darker, and she is right about the snowstorm.

'Tanveer isn't back yet.'

'He's probably chasing the chitta,' Zahid says. There is something in his eyes that Shahana can't read. He is angry with her over the militant again, she can tell, but to worry her about Tanveer unnecessarily? Zahid clearly hasn't forgiven her and Shahana doesn't know how to make it better between them.

Then his expression softens. 'He is no doubt trapping and wants to surprise us.'

'I'm going to bring him back. He's still not strong enough after being in the stream.' She races up the logs to get her shawl, socks and shoes.

Zahid follows her inside. 'I will come too.'

She isn't sure he wants to. He sounded so annoyed under the house. Maybe they should just shout at each other like normal brothers and sisters, but they are too careful. Shahana knows Zahid hides the anger he feels, and something else too, yet she knows she needs him. 'I am sorry about the militant.'

He inclines his head. 'I am too.' But Shahana knows there is more to say. The air between them is like a snow-drift, hard to see through.

'Veer has Rani with him at least,' he says. 'She is sensible.' He brings the Lee Enfield and they trudge together up the mountain. Zahid throws the rifle over his shoulder and turns, watching every direction.

They don't see Tanveer in any distance from the house that they think he could have travelled.

'Look!' Shahana thinks she sees something ahead. 'Is that Rani? Yes, we've found them.'

She hurries forward but when they reach Rani, she is alone, happily nibbling some grass she's found between patches of snow. 'Tanveer?' Shahana calls. Zahid signals to her to be quiet and checks behind the nearby trees. He looks like a soldier and Shahana's throat constricts. There is too much to think about; she must think only of Tanveer.

'The little river.' It comes out as a gasp and they both hurry down to the river's edge. 'He likes fishing here but he didn't take the net.'

Zahid checks all along the bank. 'We've been here before, trapping, but he hasn't been here today.'

'Are you sure?'

'No grass has been walked on. There are no foot-prints in the mud.'

'We will have to split up,' she says. 'I'll keep checking the forest in case he has fallen somewhere.' She gives a shaky laugh. 'Perhaps he is asleep under a tree.'

'It is too cold to fall asleep outside. I'll go down to the Neelum River.'

'You can take Rani home on the way.' Then she says, 'Be careful. The LoC runs along the river.'

'It is nearby here too.' He stands so close she thinks he will touch her. 'I don't want to leave you alone.'

'We can't be in both places at once. Look at the

weather. We must find him before the storm.'

He sighs. 'There is something you have a right to know, but I'll wait until after we find Tanveer.'

Shahana watches Zahid sliding down the mountain, leading Rani by her rope. He turns once and lifts an arm to her.

Chapter 18

Shahana has an idea. There were militants near the house and now Tanveer is gone. Doesn't that mean something? It wouldn't have been Amaan, surely, but maybe he can help. She is not sure where the militants' camp is, so she keeps climbing. They would be hidden, away from the Line of Control and the army base. Only in her dreams has she been this high up the mountain. She shrugs the thought away as the thunder of a water-fall grows closer. No wonder the little river rushes so fast – it is fed by so much power. What would it feel like to be behind that wall of water, safe from everything? She pulls her shawl around her head as she climbs. The wind is rising, and it's bitterly cold.

Then she hears the *bratatat* of automatic gunfire. There are no cries of terror or pain. Maybe she has found the camp and the men are practising their shooting. She follows the sound. Smoke from campfires rises, and she can smell the burning of chinar wood.

She stands, undecided, wondering how to proceed.

Who will she ask for? Will it go badly for Amaan if she asks for him? But it is only Amaan she wants to see. She stands behind a tree and watches. There are men with ammunition belts curling across their chests, rifles over their shoulders the way Zahid wears Nana-ji's. Most wear turbans like Amaan and some wear caps that look almost Kashmiri. Snow is falling heavily now, and they move into huts.

Suddenly she is grabbed from behind. She opens her mouth to scream but a hand presses against her face.

'Kharmosh, quiet.' The voice is familiar.

She is turned around and she sees Amaan. She stares at him in shock as he takes his hands from her. 'Little sister, I am sorry to frighten you but I was sent to intercept a spy. Can that be you?'

She finds her voice. 'I am not spying. I came to find you.'

'Then you are fortunate. I am the one they send on errands.'

There is shouting from the camp and his voice changes. 'You mustn't come here. Never come again. It is too dangerous. The men are wolves and so am I when I am with them.'

'I came because Tanveer is missing. Is he here?'

'What are you talking about? Why would he be here?'

'Militants take boys for training. I just thought—'

'You think I would do that? To your brother?'

His eyes are making her cry. 'No, not you, but there were militants near our house today and now he is gone.

115

I thought someone else might have – that you could help—'

Another shout comes from the camp.

'You have to go. It is not safe for you or for me. I will say you escaped. I will fire, but not at you. You understand?' She tips her head and snow falls off her shawl. 'I hope you find your brother. Chello, go. Now!' He fires the Kalashnikov and the sound ricochets through the trees.

Shahana runs. His gunfire is the saddest she has ever heard. She keeps running, and sobbing, afraid the other men will pursue her. She rests awhile but can't stop weeping. It is so dark now, and the snowfall so heavy, that she can't see which way is home.

'Shahana! Where are you?'

It must be Zahid. She runs towards the sound of his voice. Maybe he has found Tanveer and she can forget this horrible day. She runs into him and he holds her steady.

'Where have you been so high up the mountain? I heard shooting.'

'Looking for Tanveer. Have you found him?' But she can tell by his face that he hasn't. Her sobs start again. 'What can we do?'

'We shall go home and work out a plan.'

'But what if he is out here in the snow? What if he fell, is unconscious? What if he gets so cold he dies?'

'Come. You'll feel better after some tea and bread.'

But Shahana knows she will never feel better – not until they find Tanveer.

'We can tell others to help us look for him.'

Amaan knows; would he look for him? Shahana stops her crying. Was Amaan just pretending to be cruel to save her from the eyes of the other men?

'You are so far from home up here. There's the LoC—'

Shahana turns to see the shadow of the fence against the darkening sky.

He stops and listens.

'What is it?'

'That noise.'

'What noise?' Then she hears it too: a rumbling, like thunder in the mountain. At first she thinks it is the waterfall but remembers it is too far away. Then she realises. 'Run!' she screams. 'The snow is falling off the mountain.'

It is difficult to see which way is best. Which is the shortest route to the house? Which way will lead them into the snow's path?

'Here,' Zahid says after they can't run any more. 'Hide behind this fir tree. Its trunk is wide.' He stands behind her and puts his arms around her to hold her still. They can feel the rumbling through their feet. Shahana's whole body is shaking with the sound of growling snow.

When the snow hits the tree it holds for some moments. *Maybe we will be safe after all*, she thinks. Then the weight of the snow snaps a branch, then another. The tree groans. Zahid tightens his grip on Shahana's waist as they are swept away with the snow.

—o—o—o—

Shahana doesn't know where they are – she can see nothing. Are they at the river?

Then she feels something pricking her back. Wire. It is a fence. It must be the Line of Control. Even a wall of snow can't destroy the Line of Control.

'Zahid?' There is no answer. She can't stand. There is snow just above her. All around her are the branches of the tree; they must be holding the snow up. She feels like a pine cone hanging on a branch in a storm. She mightn't be able to see but she knows she must be cold. People die when they are buried by snow. She feels the panic rising, takes great gulps of air in an effort to steady the thunder in her chest.

She remembers Nana-ji saying people can keep warm in snow if it is all around them with a pocket of air. Zahid said Eskimos live in ice houses. She tries to calm herself.

When she touches her face the tips of her fingers are sticky, but she can't feel any pain. She moves from side to side trying to feel for Zahid. She rises to a crouch and crawls a few paces. It is as if she and the branches are in a bubble.

'Zahid.' She calls his name but the silence is an overwhelming blanket deadening any noise. She stretches her arm further and her elbow touches shoes. Zahid. She moves her hand up – it must be him.

She wonders how deep the snow is. Are they buried alive? Or could they burrow out? They have no tools. Their hands would be bloody pulp in minutes. She manages to crawl closer to Zahid. How long before the air runs out? She takes hold of his shoulders and shakes him. She touches his face; only one finger can feel his closed eyes. Then she lets her hand rest on his chest, just as she did that first night he was in the house. She can't feel whether it is rising or not so she lays her head on it instead. Would she dare to do this if he were awake?

She sits up. 'Zahid. You must wake.'

This time he moves slightly and moans. He was standing behind her – he has sheltered her and taken the force of the snow. She moves her body closer and tries to get her whole body next to his. They have to lie together – there is no other way to keep warm, to survive. She lies beside him and puts her shawl over them both. She prays he will wake; she doesn't want to die alone. At least there is one thing to be thankful for: Tanveer isn't with them. Now she is glad they didn't find him. Wherever he is, she hopes he is faring better than her.

Chapter 19

Shahana was cold. She pulled the blanket closer. She spread it to cover Tanveer as well, but he wasn't there. She crept off the charpoy and peered out the door. He must have gone outside. But snow was falling – it was the blinding, driving kind that buried villages. She ran outside without putting on her shawl.

'Tanveer,' she shouted. 'Where are you?' Her voice echoed around the mountains, which stood silently clothed in snow. Then she saw a speck high on the tallest mountain. Tanveer. She flew like a bird to reach him. The mist swirled and suddenly she was there, but the huge fence loomed up between them and she couldn't reach him. She knelt in the snow, shouting through the coils of razor wire. 'Why are you up here, Tanveer?'

'I was chasing the chitta, but I am too cold now.' He closed his eyes.

'No, stay awake!' she screamed.

Mr Nadir was right behind her. 'I told you I could look after him better than you. See, you have let him die.' And when Shahana looked at Tanveer's face, it flickered and became Zahid's.

Shahana shakes herself awake. She mustn't go to sleep, and she must wake Zahid or he will be like he was in the dream, frozen to death. She manages to sit up and shakes him. 'Zahid. Zahid!' Her words turn into sobs. She wishes she could see. Maybe he is injured. At least he is not dead. She can feel some warmth coming from him.

Then she hears his voice. 'Shahana.' It is barely a whisper.

'Zahid. You have to wake up. Now is not the time to sleep.'

He groans.

'Can you move? Come, sit with me.' She tries to pull him but she doesn't have the same strength as the day she and Tanveer dragged him home in the net.

Zahid makes an effort. 'We are trapped?'

Shahana has to lean close to hear him. 'Ji. There is snow all around us.' She doesn't say what she is thinking: that there is no way out.

He is leaning on her; he doesn't seem to be able to sit unaided. She doesn't mind. At least he is sitting up, so it will be harder for him to sleep. She talks to keep him awake.

'You said you had something to tell me.'

'Hmm?'

'In the forest you said I had the right to know something.'

He murmurs but Shahana doesn't understand.

'In Urdu, tell me in Urdu.'

'Ji.'

'Are your eyes open? Zahid, open your eyes.'

'I can't see anything.'

'Just keep them open. You mustn't go back to sleep.'

'You're bossy...like a monkey.'

'Talk to me, Zahid.' Then she adds, 'I'm frightened.'

He straightens himself at this.

'Do you hurt anywhere, Zahid?'

'Not sure.'

She knows what he means. She can't feel why her hands are sticky either.

'I wanted to tell you—' He stops, sighs and starts again. 'When I came...it was not my choosing. When I went out in the village...militants were there. Fighting the soldiers...' He stops, struggling to breathe.

'Chup, you don't have to tell me.'

'I do...the militants brought me...to Azad Kashmir. They were training me. I didn't care...maybe I could take revenge...for what soldiers did to my family and Kashmir...didn't know what it would be like...' He pauses again to catch his breath.

Shahana says gently, 'What was it like?'

'The militants wanted to kill soldiers and didn't care...who else they blew up with them.' He coughs and Shahana puts her arm around him to support him.

'Chup, quiet now.'

But he ignores her. 'They took me to a village in Kashmir. The Indian army had a base…civilians living there. The militants set bombs…destroyed the base…it wasn't all they destroyed…' He gasps as though seeing it again. 'I tripped over a child's body…a baby's leg…nightmare. I couldn't stay…'

'So you escaped.'

'I don't know how. No one escapes from a militants' camp except by a bullet. They don't stomach cowards.'

Shahana is quick. 'You are not a coward. You stayed with us even when you knew the militants were on the mountain.'

'They are the same group…Amaan was on guard duty the night I ran.'

Shahana drew in her breath. 'Amaan?'

'…when he saw me on the mountain with Tanveer …he recognised me.'

No wonder Zahid was so frightened of the militants. They would not only have taken him with them, they may have killed him.

'I…was worried he would punish you for concealing me.'

Shahana is silent. So Amaan knew all along. Why did he call her honest? Why give her money? Why did he let her go when she went to the militants' camp? Surely he wouldn't know where Zahid lived, unless he had seen him come from the house? But he has seen Zahid with Tanveer.

Zahid speaks again, a little stronger this time. 'I am sorry…can you overlook…I couldn't tell you…

123

I thought you would send me away. No one likes foreign soldiers occupying their country, or militants ... and that is what I was.'

'Why did you stay?'

'I wanted to keep you safe ... you are alone. I wanted to do good for a change.' He sighs. 'I didn't want to lose someone else.'

Shahana hears the catch in his voice and she understands. She thinks of how Tanveer will feel when he finds out what has happened to her.

'My friends idolised the militants ... wanted to join them, but the good things they said ... not all true.'

Amaan rises in her mind, his troubled frown, those clear, piercing eyes. Was he only trying to find Zahid? Did she imagine his care? He had named her his little sister. He even said so when she went to the camp. What militant keen on revenge would bother with her? Or was he gaining her trust so she would betray Zahid?

He has become too quiet. She bumps him. 'Zahid.'

'Ji.'

She has to keep him awake. 'Tell me how you came to be by the river. You said you swam across.'

'Not true.' He sounds as if he is drifting away. He is heavier on her shoulder.

'What happened? At the river?'

'The river ...' he murmurs, '... trying to cross over to Kashmir. I didn't use the bridge – check posts – couldn't swim ... river too strong ... dumped me back ...'

'And we found you.'

'Did I thank you?' He shifts his weight and his voice

changes. 'I would have liked to marry…a girl like you, Shahana.'

She thinks how sad it is that he only says this because he knows they will die.

He has fallen quiet and nothing she tries rouses him. All his weight slumps onto her shoulder and he slips to the ground. She lies beside him. It is more difficult to breathe. She will never find out what has happened to Tanveer. She will never live with Ayesha, or marry, or hold a baby in her arms. She can only pray.

Maybe dying is just like falling asleep. Zahid will feel no pain; he is already unconscious.

She hears the wild dogs barking. Now she is glad that Zahid is asleep. If the dogs manage to dig them out, will they kill them quickly or can she possibly escape? The only way she could escape from the dogs is to leave Zahid to them. How can she do that?

She sits up slowly and feels for a loose branch.

Chapter 20

The dogs are scrabbling in the snow. She and Zahid mustn't be buried too deep after all if she can hear them so close. Her hand tightens on the branch. Zahid won't wake up; she will have to protect him as well as she is able. Then she hears a voice. It is a strong voice of authority. 'Is there anyone in there? Hello? Koi hai? Is anyone there?'

Shahana opens her mouth to speak but she starts to cry instead.

'Strange, the dogs usually know.'

The voice gets further away and she does the only thing she can think of: she bangs the branch against the snow.

The dogs bark, loud and excited.

The voice returns. 'Koi hai?'

There are more voices now, and they argue.

'We are here,' Shahana finally calls. 'Help us!'

'Shhh!' Someone is shushing the dogs. There is silence outside and she says it again.

'We are here.'

The voices start up again; shovels bite against the snow. Shahana shakes Zahid. 'Wake up, wake up.' But he doesn't stir.

'Please hurry,' she shouts.

There is more arguing, then the noise of a vehicle, coming closer, then moving away. Driving close again.

The dogs bark constantly now. For men to be there the dogs must be trained. She wonders who the men are. There are voices behind her now too, speaking a language she doesn't know.

She can see lights through the snow ahead of her. She uses the branch to push the snow away. Someone is shovelling from the other side and he breaks through. She feels the chilled air burst onto her face and she gasps and sobs. Hands reach in to draw her out. The first thing she notices is the clear night air; it has stopped snowing.

'Zahid—' She starts to say her brother is with her and stops herself in time. 'My cousin is there too.' She sees a khaki camouflage uniform and looks up into the face of a Pakistani army officer. There are two dogs. Another officer calls them to heel and they sit with their tongues lolling, as if they are happy with a job well done. Shahana has never been glad to see a dog before. A soldier is lying on the ground and a man in uniform is tending to him.

'You are fortunate that a soldier was caught in the avalanche,' says the man who has pulled her out.

There is a commotion from behind the heap of snow. Shahana can see that it is large, although not as big as one she saw late last winter when the snow began to melt on the mountain.

A weapon is fired. The army men ready their assault rifles. The officer shouts, 'We will keep to the ceasefire tonight. All we are doing is rescuing those caught in the avalanche.'

The men all lower their rifles and militants emerge from behind the mound of snow. They look so burly and fiery, even more so than Amaan. One of them says, 'You have lost an opportunity. There are Indian soldiers digging out their men on the other side. We can pick them off for you while the LoC electricity is down.'

Then Shahana sees Amaan pulling Zahid out from the snow. Her chest slumps. One word from Amaan and the militants will take Zahid away. What can she do? She crawls over to Amaan to plead for Zahid but another militant is there too.

'Isn't this that Kashmiri kid we had training with us?' the other militant asks.

Amaan glances at Shahana. She is about to beg him to save them, but he shakes his head slightly, warning her to stay silent.

'No,' he says.

'Are you sure? You had the most to do with him.'

Shahana remembers Zahid's words in the snow. *Amaan knew him, but does he know he is the boy Shahana calls her brother?*

Amaan peers into Zahid's face. It is as pale as bread flour. 'Nothing like him.'

'He is my relative,' Shahana manages to say through her tears. 'He is just a jawan, a teenage boy.'

Amaan looks over at the army officer. 'Can you help him? These kids are orphans of the war, they have no money for a doctor.'

The officer looks at Amaan in surprise, but he lifts his hand and barks an order. Two young men carrying a stretcher materialise. Shahana wonders at such authority that can make things happen with just a word.

Shahana is not sure she wants Zahid to go to the army barracks. The militants are kind to help the army dig out victims but she's heard rumours that the army watches them carefully in case they make trouble. And what if the army finds out Zahid has been with the militants?

The officer comes to kneel by Shahana. 'I am a doctor. I will bandage your hands.'

She looks down and sees the blood. She hasn't noticed before.

'You can feel pain?' he asks.

'Nay, janab.'

Amaan is standing close by, watching.

The doctor asks to see her feet. 'Fortunately you were not buried long enough to lose toes.'

'Can I go with my cousin?' she asks.

'No, you may not come to the army base. You are well enough to return home. Some men from your village are here. Is there anyone you know who can take you home?'

She sees a little bulldozer with a soldier in the seat.

Then she sees men from the village leaning on shovels beside it. So they have helped. They have seen Zahid pulled out of the snow. Have they heard her call him her relative? She recognises Mr Pervaiz and points at him. 'That one.'

An army officer calls him over. 'You know this girl?'

'Ji, janab. I will look after her and take her to the village.'

'How will I know if my cousin is well enough to come home?' she says softly to the doctor.

He is quiet while he finishes her bandages and she worries why he won't answer her. Even Nana-ji, for all his honesty, wouldn't admit if someone was about to die. The doctor looks at her before he answers. 'We will let you know, when he recovers.'

Shahana hears the way the doctor hesitates over the word *when*, but she lifts her chin and tries to speak firmly, as her mother would. 'I will wait for your message, doctor sahib. I will be at the half-widow's house, Mrs Habib Sheikh.' She gives Aunty Rabia's formal name.

Amaan is regarding her, but he waits for the other militants to leave before he speaks. 'Have you found your young brother? Was he with you—' He leaves the rest unsaid.

'Nay,' she says. 'I do not know where he is.'

'Then I will search also.' Amaan glances at Mr Pervaiz and nods. He is so stern, as if he doesn't care for her at all, yet he has lied to save Zahid's life. Why has he helped them?

Shahana cannot walk, so Mr Pervaiz lifts her onto his back. She looks behind her and sees Amaan, like a man carved in stone, facing her way. Behind him, above the mountains, the sky is lightening in the east.

Chapter 21

Shahana wakes in a strange bed yet she can hear Rani bleating outside. Someone is lying beside her. Tanveer? She lifts her head to check. It is Ayesha. She is breathing softly, her mouth slightly open, her shut eyes flickering slightly. How peaceful she looks.

Shahana wonders if Tanveer has woken. What she wouldn't give to see him breathing softly beside her like this. She squeezes her eyes shut. Where hasn't she looked for him? The Neelum River? But Zahid said he wasn't there. It was getting dark by then, could Zahid have seen clearly? Or was Tanveer still on the mountain under a pile of snow or branches? And what of Zahid? She lets out a groan.

'Shahana?' Ayesha's hand is on her arm. 'How do you feel today?'

What can she say?

Ayesha stretches and rolls over onto her elbows. 'When Mr Pervaiz brought you last night you were so tired we just put you on the bed. But he said something about a boy. That the army took him. Was that Tanveer? Is that why he isn't with you?'

Shahana closes her eyes. 'I lost Tanveer.'

'Lost him? You mean in the avalanche? They didn't dig him out?'

Shahana starts as if she's seen a jinn. Could that have happened? Was he rolled along with the snow too? But the dogs would have found him. She tries to calm herself.

'Nay, he went to gather wood just like he always does. We found Rani, but not Tanveer. We went everywhere – the rivers, I even went right up the mountain. That is what Zahid and I were doing when we were caught in the snow. We were looking for Tanveer.'

The tears roll down her face and Ayesha sits up to put her arms around her. 'I am so sorry to hear that.'

'He must be still out there. There were trained dogs at the snow, but they didn't find Tanveer.' She says this aloud for her own benefit, to stop thinking of useless possibilities. 'I must keep searching for him.'

'Your hands need to heal. And you were cramped up for so long in the cold that you'll need practice walking.'

'I can do that searching for Tanveer.'

Ayesha sighs. 'I will come with you. Though if there were dogs wouldn't they have found him if he was on the mountain?'

'What if he wasn't in their path?' Then a frightening thought came to her. What if the wild dogs found him?

She pulls back the quilt. She is wearing a clean

shalwar qameez. Ayesha smiles at her. 'You were so wet last night that Ummie and I washed you with hot water before you fell asleep.'

'I don't remember.'

'I am not surprised.'

Then Ayesha says, 'So it was the boy, Zahid, the army took. Why? Did they think he was a fugitive?'

'I hope not. He was unconscious. The army doctor took him to their clinic.' What if the army does find out Zahid was being trained as a militant? Would they put him in prison or in the refugee camp? She won't tell Ayesha what he told her in the snow. Shahana has noticed how she hesitated over his name: Ayesha doesn't trust him. But did she herself trust him in the beginning? Wouldn't she have sent him away if he told her at the start he was a boy militant?

'Shahana? I am so sorry for your trouble. It is very difficult for you, and I will help you.' Then Ayesha says thoughtfully, 'What about Mr Nadir?'

'What about him?' Shahana turns to look at her. She doesn't want to think about him right now; there is too much to worry about. *The dupatta.* She touches her bandages. 'I won't be able to finish the dupatta now. Will you tell him?'

'We could both go.'

It is Ayesha's tone; it is as if she knows something. 'What are you thinking?' Shahana asks.

'Did he ever offer Tanveer work?'

'Yes, knotting carpets, but I refused. I would never be able to pay him out again.' Shahana pauses, watching

134

Ayesha's face and following her thoughts. 'Surely he wouldn't just take him?'

'Maybe not him, but someone else may have abducted Tanveer and taken him to Mr Nadir. Times are hard because of the conflict, especially in winter.'

'But Mr Nadir would have to ask me, give me money. Nothing like that has happened.'

'He might have if it wasn't for the avalanche. Now everyone will say Tanveer died in it.'

'How can you say that?'

'Don't be upset with me, I don't think he died. But do you not think it is strange that he went missing not far from your house?'

Shahana remembers the men who came past the house. Was it possible they weren't militants, just some men in need of money? Has she mistaken men for militants, just as the Indian soldiers did with her father? Just like the king who acted first and asked questions later in that old story.

If Ayesha is right then Mr Nadir would have paid the men for Tanveer to work on his loom. 'Would Mr Nadir think I sent the men?'

'That is possible.'

'If it's true, how will we free him?'

'First we have to find out if he's there.'

Shahana's thoughts are raging like the river in flood after the snow melts. If it is true, then Tanveer at least is alive. She won't have to worry about him being eaten by wolves or leopards or dying of cold because she couldn't find him in time. But if it is true, will she be able to release him? He'll be so frightened he won't be able to breathe. What if Mr Nadir doesn't know what medicine to give him? One thing Shahana does know: Mr Nadir will never give Tanveer back just because she and Ayesha ask him to.

'Let's hope Mr Nadir does have him,' Ayesha says.

'Why?'

'Because we at least know Mr Nadir. If he has sent Tanveer somewhere else, it will be harder to find him.'

Somewhere else? It is too awful to consider. 'Maybe he fell in the stream.' She wishes she didn't sound so hopeless.

Ayesha says gently, 'You have already looked and there was no sign.'

'I am being foolish, but it is a terrifying thing to think of Mr Nadir having Tanveer.' Shahana stands up and wobbles on her feet. She ignores the pain shooting down her legs and thinks of what her mother and nana would say. Her mother would say God will help her. Then she hears Nana-ji's voice in her head. *Once you have faced the impossible, there is only the possible left.* Hasn't she faced the impossible in the snow? She thought she would die.

She turns to Ayesha and holds out her hand. 'Can you help me walk to the kitchen? I will make roti for breakfast with you.' She wants to be strong enough to stride into Mr Nadir's shop like an army colonel when they go to find Tanveer.

Chapter 22

When Shahana was born there was fighting across the Line of Control. It was near the end of the first sister of winter and the fir forest caught fire from the shelling and rockets. Her father called her his fire queen, for Shahana means 'queen'. 'Precious things are made strong in fire,' he would say to Shahana. It was to remind her to be strong and not despair. 'One day you will be Shahana on fire and you will shine for your family.'

Shahana can't think of anything she has done that she would consider being Shahana on fire. Looking after Tanveer is a good thing to do but losing him isn't. Right now Ayesha says it is a good thing just to practise walking around their house. The pain in her legs is getting less and she can now walk without Ayesha holding her hand. She wonders how Zahid is and when the doctor will tell her he can come home. She will have to stay at Ayesha's house but Zahid could live in Nana-ji's house. Every time she thinks about Tanveer her heart shudders and bangs. There is nothing she can do to stop it.

After some days Ayesha takes Shahana's bandages off and replaces them with special tape. Now Shahana has the tips of her fingers to use. She manages to go down the steps to milk Rani. Aunty Rabia has a hut that Rani sleeps in. The milking is soothing and gives Shahana time to think, though some things are too difficult to contemplate. If Ayesha is right about Tanveer, what can they do? Mr Nadir is an important businessman. What if Zahid doesn't get better? And Amaan? If he knew about Zahid the whole time why did he lie to save him? Was it only because she had asked him to protect the boys?

Shahana brings the milk inside and puts it by the stove. She stands there, wondering what to do next. Without embroidery to sew or Tanveer to look after she can't think of anything constructive to do, so she keeps Aunty Rabia company watching TV. A Kashmiri documentary begins, showing women sitting in a park with signs written in Angrezi.

'Ayesha,' Shahana calls, 'come, look at this.'

She checks that Aunty Rabia is watching too. 'Aunty-ji, this is a special program.'

A young Kashmiri woman, not unlike the one Shahana saw on the TV in the teashop, tells how there are so many missing persons. She talks about the stigma of having a missing family member and then shows the women in the park in Srinagar. She explains that they sit there once a month to ask the government to do something about the missing people.

'See, Ummie-ji,' Ayesha says. 'There are many people like us. They are sad but they are not ashamed to sit in a park to let the world know about this injustice.'

The young woman interviews a mother with a sign. 'I have lost all my sons and my husband,' the mother says in Kashmiri as Urdu writing on the bottom of the screen translates what she is saying. 'I do not have their bodies – I cannot bury them. Why are there so many missing people? If they are in prison, let them out. If they have died in prison, tell the families.'

The interviewer sits in a car and is driven almost to the Line of Control near Azad Kashmir. She gets out of the car and speaks to the camera. 'There are many unmarked graves here.' The camera shows an unkempt grave. Aunty Rabia gives a cry. 'Families have not been told where their loved ones are. We shall ask the right government groups to act on this.' There are thousands of graves, derelict, as if all the people in the country have died and there is no one left to tend them. To Shahana it looks like the end of the world. 'Even though many people do not put a special stone on their loved one's grave,' says the interviewer, 'at least they mark where it is with a simple name plate.'

Aunty Rabia sobs. 'Yes, everyone should know where their loved ones are.'

'Abu may still be alive, Ummie-ji,' Ayesha says softly.

'And he may not be,' Aunty Rabia says. 'But we will do something about it now.'

'What will we do?' Ayesha asks.

Aunty Rabia takes a shuddering breath and stops weeping. 'We will make our own signs. We will send them by email. We will put one outside our house. No one will say my brave husband is a coward. They will understand he has been taken.'

Shahana thinks of Zahid and wonders if his mother is with those women. Does she believe Zahid is dead too, and that she has no body to bury?

Ayesha gives her mother some paper and a pencil. Aunty Rabia and Shahana sit on carpet cushions and Ayesha brings the computer in.

'We can work on our stories,' she says to Shahana.

'I need to find Tanveer,' Shahana says. How can a story help her do that?

'The story may not bring Tanveer back but it might make you feel better and it can let others know what is happening,' Ayesha says as she waits for the website to appear.

Shahana is not sure she agrees, but she watches the page flicker on the screen as Ayesha starts typing. She is writing a story about her father, saying that half-widows should not be called names and the innocent prisoners should be set free. She reads sentences out to Shahana but Shahana cannot concentrate. She wants to write how hard it is to be a mother and how she didn't mean to lose Tanveer. But how can she put that shame onto a screen for everyone to see? Ayesha glances at her and Shahana drops her head to write on the paper. She wants someone to help her but by the time her story is ready to go on the website it may be too late for Tanveer. Shahana's hand stills. She knows what she will do; she is ready. She will go to Mr Nadir's tomorrow and try to find out if he has Tanveer.

Ayesha puts a CD in the computer and music fills the room. Shahana can't concentrate on her story now – not with her decision weighing on her mind and the song filling her with memories of a happier time. It is from a movie she saw at Ayesha's house years ago.

The movie is about a blind Kashmiri girl, Zooni, who falls in love with a freedom fighter, though authorities call him a terrorist. The final scene takes place in the snow. The girl has shot him so he can't fulfil his mission. Shahana wonders how Zooni could do that.

Shahana would protect Tanveer no matter what happened. She is thinking of Zahid as well. Even Amaan didn't hand Zahid over to the militants. How difficult it is to make choices, to decide what is right or wrong. If Shahana could find a way to keep Tanveer safe she wouldn't care what it cost: it would be the right choice if it saved Tanveer.

Ayesha pulls her orange dupatta off and throws it in the air like Zooni did in the movie. It looks like autumn leaves falling. Shahana watches it billow over Ayesha's head as she dances around. '*When you're close, this world is naught, destroyed in your love, a triumph sought. May my life's breath find refuge in your heart.*' Ayesha laughs and pulls Shahana up by her waist. She sings the words again and swings Shahana around. Shahana manages to stay on her feet.

She knows Ayesha is trying to cheer her up with the song but it only makes her think about Zahid, how she put her hand on his chest and hardly felt his heart beat at all. If only her breath could have found refuge in his heart.

Chapter 23

Shahana was in the snow, looking for the leopard. She wanted to ask if it had seen Tanveer. She climbed up the mountain near the stream. The water was iced over but she could see the fish swimming underneath, as if the ice was glass. She knelt on the bank. Something bigger was floating by. A huge fish? No, it was a body. She saw the feet first. A child. Then she saw his face. It was Tanveer. He was caught under the ice. His eyes were open and he could see her. His hands were up against the ice, trying to push his way out. His mouth opened wide, as if he were screaming.

Shahana snaps awake, panting.

'Are you okay?' Ayesha is lying on her side watching her. 'You were calling for Tanveer.'

'I had a terrible dream. I have so many, but this one – he could see me and I could do nothing. I couldn't break the ice. Oh, Ayesha. What will I do? He needs me, I know it.' She pauses. 'I have to see Mr Nadir.'

'We will go together.'

'But what will we say? We can't just ask for Tanveer back.' *And what if he doesn't have him?*

'We mustn't say much at all. We will see how he reacts when he sees us. We will just say that you can't sew yet.'

Shahana examines the tape on her hands. It is less constricting than the bandages. Now she can do everything for herself except sew. 'I'll take this off soon, but we'll leave it on for Mr Nadir.'

'Good idea.'

They walk slowly down the steps, careful not to slip. A narrow pathway on the bazaar road has been cleared of snow, but it is banked up high on either side of the road. They pass Mr Pervaiz on the way. It feels so long since Shahana has been in the bazaar. She exchanges greetings with Mr Pervaiz. 'Thank you for bringing me home from the avalanche.'

'Are you better now?'

'Ji, thank you. Aunty Rabia is looking after me well.' Actually, it is mainly Ayesha, but it is polite to mention Aunty Rabia.

Mr Pervaiz tips his head and smiles at them. 'If there is anything you need help with, don't hesitate to ask me.'

The girls glance at each other and Ayesha says, 'Thank you, janab.' Then she adds, in a voice so casual it sounds like she is talking about the snow, 'We are just going to see Mr Nadir. If we don't come out in a short while, can you please come to ask for us?'

Mr Pervaiz looks as if he doesn't know what to say. He glances at Mr Nadir's shop then back at the girls. 'Are you in some kind of trouble?'

'We hope not,' Ayesha says, but Shahana can't keep the tears from her eyes. Mr Pervaiz must have noticed, but he doesn't remark on it.

'Zarur, certainly, I will always watch out for you.' He is looking at Shahana as he says this. She wonders if he has questions about her behaviour – he must know about Zahid. She hopes no one else in the bazaar does.

Mr Nadir is writing in a book on the counter when they enter the shop. Shahana feels as though she is walking into a wild dog's lair.

'Assalamu alaikum,' Shahana says.

Mr Nadir nods his head but doesn't bother to return the greeting.

'I have come to say I cannot sew. My hands were injured in the avalanche.'

Mr Nadir purses his lips as he stares at Shahana's hands. Then he says, 'I hear you have lost your little brother. That's rather remiss of you, is it not?'

Ayesha gives a gasp. 'How can you be so cruel?'

'Cruel? I'm sure the little boy is being looked after better than he's ever been.'

Ayesha narrows her eyes at him. 'You have him, don't you? That's how you know he is missing.'

Shahana's mouth opens in shock. In less than a minute Ayesha has forgotten how circumspect they must be.

Mr Nadir stares at them both, a smile curling around his lips. 'Actually, I paid a man who brought him to me.' He turns to Shahana. 'He didn't give the money to you? Such a charlatan.'

144

'But he can't be sold. I didn't give my permission.'

'Oh yes, you did.' He pushes over a piece of paper.

On it is a word she doesn't understand and something about a loan. Shahana sees a signature. 'This is not my writing.'

'It gives your name, and mine is here. Look.'

Shahana doesn't want to look. 'I didn't do this.'

'You must have been hurt quite badly in the avalanche if you don't remember, my dear. The man said you had explained how difficult it is to look after him now it is winter and you have no money.'

'But Tanveer is sick and needs medicine. I would never give him up.'

Mr Nadir smiles at her. 'He is growing into a little man with me, not being turned into a baby by you.'

'His lungs are weak. He needs to keep warm. If the air is too cold he wheezes.'

'That's a little unfortunate in this village, don't you think?' Mr Nadir adds, 'I had to pay a lot – it's a pity you haven't seen any of it. Unless you don't remember that either.' Ayesha snorts, but Mr Nadir carries on. 'The boy ties knots so well, and can keep a pattern better than the others. I would need so much more money than I paid to let him go.' Then he says, 'I may even have to move him to a better factory so he can show his true talent.'

Shahana clutches hold of the counter and Ayesha puts an arm around her. If Mr Nadir moves Tanveer she'll never find him.

Ayesha cuts in then. 'You should do the decent thing and give him back to her.' She scowls at him.

'Yes,' Shahana says. She hates the way her voice sounds wobbly. 'There's been a mistake. Those men stole him, and I have no way of buying him back.'

Mr Nadir is silent a moment but he looks pleased. Too pleased. What has she said?

He turns so he is looking just at Shahana. 'But you do have something you can give to me. Have you forgotten that as well?'

Shahana frowns at him, wondering what he could mean. The house? It is the only thing she owns.

'When your hands are better, of course.'

'Sewing?' How could she do enough embroidery to pay off Tanveer's bondage?

Mr Nadir speaks as though he hasn't heard her. 'Though, it might be difficult to make a bargain now, since your cousin was with you in the avalanche.' He says 'cousin' as if he means 'lover'.

She stares at him in horror. *The proposal.* And he knows about Zahid. She gasps as if she has run out of air. 'But I refused.'

Mr Nadir shrugs. 'It is your choice I suppose. Truly, your brother is better off with me. My business will grow and there will be many opportunities. With his skill he could be the manager of my shop by the time he is twenty.'

Shahana tries not to show how devastated she is, but her legs betray her and she slumps against the counter. This is not the life she wants for Tanveer – sitting at a loom all day when he is so young. He needs the fresh air, the sun, for his lungs. She wants him to study, though she's not sure how she will manage that – she will never be able to pay for the exercise books. And there is no school anyway. She feels her air escaping, like a balloon.

It is as if Mr Nadir can read her mind. 'What benefits can you give him, na? He'll end up joining the militants. That is probably where people think he is now.'

Shahana can't answer him but Ayesha does. 'My mother can look after both Shahana and Tanveer.' Then she bites her lip as if she has said too much.

Mr Nadir looks at her with interest. 'Is that so? Well, I might notify the authorities. Shahana will be in an orphanage before she can say "salaam". I am the one who is looking after Tanveer and providing him with opportunities.'

Then he regards Shahana. His face is almost kind but she feels it is the look of a dog staring at a fowl he will be pleased to eat. 'You have only one choice really, don't you?' he says, his head tilted to one side.

She wants to accuse him of dishonesty. Even if she agrees to be married, how does she know he will keep to his bargain? Will he ever give Tanveer back once he discovers how talented he is, and that she has also taught him how to embroider?

The bell on the door jingles and Mr Pervaiz appears.

'We must go,' Ayesha says, her voice tight like a spring. 'Mr Pervaiz is taking us home.'

Shahana can't get Mr Nadir out of her head. Once Mr Pervaiz goes back to his shop and they thank him for watching over them, Ayesha speaks her mind. 'That is the first time I've seen Mr Nadir in ages. He is so

147

corrupt – making himself rich because of the conflict. You can't trust him, Shahana. You mustn't go back or do anything he asks.'

Shahana thinks how hard it all is. She remembers the movie. At the end, Zooni says it's easy to choose between right and wrong, but that to choose the greater of two goods or the lesser of two evils are the choices of our life. How many times has she, Shahana, made choices that she wouldn't have had to make if Irfan or her parents were alive? Taking Zahid home may have been an immoral choice, but she couldn't leave him to the dogs. Talking to Amaan may have been unwise, but she did it to protect Zahid and Tanveer. Right or wrong, she has broken barriers. And now she is thinking of doing something she doesn't want to do, something that would give Tanveer a better life. Isn't that a good thing?

'Shahana? Did you hear me? Don't trust him.'

Chapter 24

Shahana can walk so well she decides to go to her house, since it isn't snowing. She tells Ayesha she wants to collect her clothes, Tanveer's medicine, and also her embroidery, to see if her fingers are able to sew yet. But really she wants to search again for Tanveer. Part of her is hoping that Mr Nadir is lying, that Tanveer was just lost and has gone back to the house. He knows how to start a fire. He can make chai. He could possibly make bread, though it might taste like cardboard boxes. She smiles. *Oh Tanveer, when will I see you?* She feels the sharp pain that Aunty Rabia and Ayesha must have endured for the past two years.

'Will you be all right?' Ayesha asks. 'I have to stay with Ummie this morning, but if you wait until after lunch I can come with you.'

Shahana shakes her head. 'I will be fine. Always I have walked on the mountain by myself, or with Tanveer—'

Ayesha puts an arm around her shoulders. She

doesn't say any soothing words and Shahana is glad. Nice words are not going to bring Tanveer back, and having Tanveer back is all Shahana wants.

She makes her way out through the village and across the bridge. Someone has cleared a pathway through the snow and swept the planks on the bridge. Shahana can't walk as quickly as she used to and by the time she reaches the house, her legs are aching. She stops at the bottom of the logs. Someone has swept the snow away there, too. *Tanveer.* It must be him. It was always his job.

She hurries as best she can to the door, opens it and looks inside. 'Tanveer?'

But he isn't there. Nothing has been touched or moved since she went out that day looking for him. The reed flute is lying on the charpoy where Zahid left it. So is the dupatta she was embroidering. She picks up the carving of the camel. Tears spring to her eyes as she berates herself for having foolish hopes. She finds her backpack and puts in all the things she thinks they will need, plus the flute, Tanveer's camel and her own heart-shaped papier-mâché box. Finally, she picks up the dupatta and gold thread, thinks for a moment, then stuffs them into the bag too.

'Assalamu alaikum, sister.' The voice is outside.

She wipes her eyes and pulls her shawl over the bottom half of her face as she goes out the door. She hesitates on the logs, looking down at Amaan. He stands as he always does, his Kalashnikov slung over his shoulder, the tail of his turban hanging down his back.

'Wa alaikum assalam.' Her voice sounds flat but there is nothing she can do about it.

'You are living here again?'

'Nay, janab.'

'I was returning up the mountain; I looked back and saw you walking to your door.'

Shahana stares at him. 'You were here? You swept the snow away?'

He tips his head, as though it is not a big thing to make a fuss over. There is so much she needs to thank him for, but she doesn't know where to begin.

'I am just keeping an eye on your house until you return.'

'That is very kind,' Shahana says.

'Have you found your little brother yet?'

The tears well up again and Shahana cannot stop them; they dribble down her face. She doesn't want Amaan to see them but he takes a step up the logs. His look is caring, like her brother Irfan's was if ever she fell. 'You have no idea where he is?'

Shahana tries to blink away the tears. 'Ji nahin.' But those are just words. Her mind shows her all sorts of places where he could be: at the bottom of the Neelum River, under a snowdrift or under the ice. In Mr Nadir's poky dark room.

She takes a deep breath. 'Actually, there is a man in the village who may have him. He has a weaving loom and boys in debt bondage work it for him. He said a man sold Tanveer to him, but I don't know if he is telling the truth.'

Amaan takes another step towards her. 'This is serious, sister.'

'Ji. And I don't know what to do.'

He glances away, frowning.

'There is something he wants,' she ventures.

'And what is that?'

'He has a marriage proposal for me, from a friend of his. If I accept I think he will release Tanveer.'

Amaan is only halfway up the logs but she can hear his breathing. 'You must not accept this proposal. Men like that are foxes.'

'My friend Ayesha's mother will look after Tanveer,' Shahana continues, as if she hasn't heard Amaan's words.

His hand flashes out and almost touches her. The shawl falls from her face and he steps back, as if remembering she isn't his true sister. 'He will sell you to the highest bidder. You'll end up some old goat's third wife, or worse. You'll be a slave only.' His words are harsh but she knows it is because he cares.

She glances at him. 'What can I do?'

'The police?'

'They are in Athmuqam. It's a long way from here and I think they will listen to Mr Nadir before they will listen to me.'

'The mosque? Isn't there someone who will help you?'

Shahana thinks of the little village mosque with its rusty roof and dome of brass, and Mr Pervaiz going to prayer every Friday. 'Maybe there is a man.'

'The one who took you home the other night?'

She gives a nod. 'But if Mr Nadir thinks I am planning against him he might move Tanveer. I can't risk that. I will never find him.'

'You must not do anything until you know for sure.'

She smiles faintly at the brotherly concern. She misses Irfan telling her what to do.

'I want to thank you,' Shahana says in the silence, 'for saving us the other night. Zahid is just like a brother but he isn't and I let you think he was – I just wanted to protect them both—'

Amaan cuts into her sentence. 'You are children only. In times of conflict we survive the best we can. That is all you were doing – trying to survive.'

Shahana looks up. 'They haven't told me if Zahid is well.'

'That is because they are checking who he is.'

'But they will realise he crossed over.'

'I imagine they know that already.' He sounds as if it is a joke but nothing is funny.

'Then I must go there. Tell them—'

'No.'

She frowns at him.

He softens his voice. 'I already have.'

'Why would you do that?' What a risk to take, to walk into a cave where a leopard has cubs.

'At the avalanche, they heard what Abdul said about him being with us, so I went to explain.'

'What did you say?'

'The same as I said that night – I didn't recognise him.'

153

Would they believe him? There is no love between the army and the militants.

'Thank you.'

He looks at her in surprise. 'I promised.'

'Ji, and I am grateful you remembered.'

'How could I not?' He blows out a breath. Shahana has never seen him look unsure before.

He glances at her. 'Zahid reminds me of myself. I want to leave, do something that brings life. Zahid felt the same, I believe. I suspected he'd try to escape. Fortunately, he did so when I was on watch. I let him go. Just fired over his head.'

'Like you did with me?'

'I have a name in the camp for being a poor shot.' It is a joke, but his eyes do not glisten. 'They may think I am too involved with the local people – that I am becoming soft.'

Shahana wonders if he is in trouble because of her.

'I followed his tracks the next day to check he got across the LoC. It is difficult now, with the razor wire and mines. He didn't have the stamina expected in a jawan.'

It is the way he is looking at her, as if he is trying to tell her something important, and she thinks of that morning – the net, the wild dogs. 'You,' she whispers. 'You shot the dog?'

He bows his head slightly and lays his hand over his heart.

She stares at him, trying not to think how Amaan reminds her of her father at that moment, and how she wishes he were still here.

'Can you come with me to Mr Nadir?' There, she has said it, but she doesn't realise what she has asked. She can only think of Tanveer in a dark room, tying knots all day and not being able to breathe.

'It is difficult,' he says. 'The people will tolerate us in the mountains out of sight, but they will not like to see me in the village. Do you understand this?'

She thinks of the day Irfan and her mother died. A different group of militants were in the village that day. She has hated militants ever since, but she doesn't hate Amaan. She wants to tell him this, but isn't sure how.

'I can understand why the people hate us,' he says. It is as if her thoughts are plain to see on her face. 'But they might want revenge and more people will get hurt. I understand revenge. It is what my family lives by. Revenge makes you strong and keeps the peace.'

Shahana used to want revenge against the militants too, but just by caring for her and Zahid and Tanveer, Amaan has taught her to let it go. The thought makes her smile. She doubts he would want to hear what she is thinking.

'So you are happy now, little sister?'

How disconcerting he is. His voice has a laugh in it, even though he is not smiling. Is she wrong to trust him? She is tired of second-guessing, wondering who is trustworthy. Before her parents died she never had to think about such things.

Instead, she asks about Zahid. 'When you went to the army base, was Zahid well?'

He hesitates only slightly but Shahana notices.

155

'I didn't see him but he is alive. They said he will soon be able to leave.'

This is good news. Shahana wants to see Zahid for herself. 'How will I get news to you if I need to?'

'Leave a message here, under your house. I will come sometimes.' He steps backwards. 'Khuda hafiz.'

She wants to say healing words before he leaves. She may not see him again. 'Amaan-ji.' It is the first time she has used his name and it makes him pause. He turns to look at her. 'You have taught me something. You have helped me to forgive.'

He lowers his gaze and gives a small smile, but it is not for her. When he lifts his head he says, 'Then I am a poor jihadi indeed, little sister.'

Chapter 25

Shahana ignores Amaan's advice and goes to find the army base. She knows she shouldn't go alone – her mother's and Nana-ji's voices both shout in her head but she ignores them too. She walks up the mountain along the Line of Control, passing the mound of snow she and Zahid were buried in, but there is still no sign of the base. She rests, then trudges further, following the razor wire until she sees huts. At first she thinks she is back at the militants' camp, but these huts have a fence around them, a fence with curled razor wire, like the Line of Control. She finds the gate. The base is smaller than she thought it would be. A soldier is sitting in a small shelter. When he sees her he stands, and points his assault rifle at her.

'What are you doing here? This is out of bounds for civilians.' His voice is rough but his gaze isn't as piercing as Amaan's.

She eyes the rifle. Could it go off by accident? The man makes an impatient movement and she takes a deep breath. She speaks as though she's been sent for. 'I've come to see the doctor. He has my cousin in the clinic.' She is satisfied to see the surprise on the man's face when she speaks Urdu.

The soldier asks her name and then talks into a two-way radio, but Shahana can't understand what he is saying, other than when he uses her name. 'Okay,' he finally says. Then he looks at Shahana. 'The doctor will see you but he is busy.' He points to a hut opposite them in the compound. 'That is the clinic. Make sure you leave immediately after you've spoken with him.'

'Ji, janab, shukriya.' Shahana is glad there are not many soldiers around. She knocks on the clinic door and waits. When the door opens, she sees the doctor in the doorway.

'Come,' he says. He doesn't smile, and Shahana feels a sudden jolt of pain. Did Amaan lie when he said that Zahid was well to save her from worrying?

'Is my cousin well?' she asks before she sits on the plastic chair the doctor gestures towards.

The doctor waits until they are both seated before he answers. 'He is as well as can be expected.'

She waits to see what this means.

'Shahana, your cousin has a heart condition. Did you know this?'

She shakes her head slightly.

'I believe he has a hole in his heart, but tests at a hospital will tell for sure.'

'A hole?' She imagines the blood rushing out of his heart into the rest of his body.

158

'He has probably always had it. When he gets older he will need an operation. It will be why he has little energy. Have you not noticed?'

Shahana thinks of when they first found him, and how he got out of breath on the mountain, how he couldn't pull Tanveer out of the stream. Did Zahid know? Was that something else he hadn't told her?

'He will be all right after the operation?' she asks.

'Yes, but it is expensive. At the moment it is only in times of extreme exertion that it will bother him. It's then that his heart doesn't pump well enough.'

'When can he come home?'

The doctor regards Shahana. 'Are you able to look after him?'

'Ji, janab.' Shahana speaks without thinking how she will do it. She can ask Mr Pervaiz.

'Actually, we need the bed, so if you can take him with you now, that will be good.' Then the doctor speaks in a lower tone. 'Shahana—'

She looks up in surprise.

'Even if Zahid is really your cousin—' He stops and Shahana feels an icy finger creep up her back. This man may be a doctor, but he is still an army officer.

'He must either apply for refugee status or leave Azad Kashmir.'

Shahana doesn't know what to say; she stares at him in shock. Will they be punished?

'How do you know?'

'Even the orderly heard him talking in Kashmiri when he was delirious. Too many people know. He is not safe.' He sighs. 'You are just children and I will not report you. Get him strong again then send him home across the LoC. Here is a travel paper so our army will let him through, as well as his medical documents for when he visits a hospital in Srinagar.'

'But the soldiers on the other side...' She leaves the sentence unfinished. Her father was on the wrong side of the Line of Control and he was shot. Why would Zahid be any safer?

'Do not worry, his travel document explains that he is visiting.' The doctor smiles. 'You'll need to give him different clothes before he crosses. In the meantime, keep him out of trouble.'

Shahana puts the envelope in her pocket as the doctor disappears through a door. When he returns, Zahid is with him. He is dressed in a Pakistani army uniform. No wonder the doctor mentioned his clothes. There are dark shadows under his eyes; he is pale, and thinner, but there is a grin on his face. He also has a plastic bag containing his clothes and Nana-ji's pheran.

'Zahid, I have come to take you home.' She tries to speak brightly, but he looks even worse than when he was recovering from being in the river the first time.

On the slow walk back to Nana-ji's house, before Shahana can tell Zahid about Tanveer, he tells her he must leave. At first she says nothing. All along she has known this would happen, but she didn't expect her heart to feel so heavy.

'Wait until you are strong enough,' she finally says.

He doesn't mention his heart, even though Shahana

is sure he must have been told. 'I think Amaan can be trusted,' she suddenly says, and she tells Zahid he is looking after the house. 'He said I can leave a note if I need him.' She doesn't tell Zahid everything, for she suspects he would not like to feel beholden to Amaan.

Zahid makes no comment and Shahana isn't sure if he is angry or just trying to negotiate the mountain path.

They don't speak again until they arrive at the site of the avalanche. Zahid searches in the snow and comes out with Nana-ji's Lee Enfield. 'Veer will need this when he is older.' And that is when she tells him where she believes Tanveer is.

'You mustn't go near this Mr Nadir. If you do he will have both of you.' He sounds just like Amaan.

'But Tanveer's lungs...' Why won't they understand she has to get him back?

Zahid says more gently. 'I haven't heard of many boys escaping bonded labour.'

'There must be something that can be done.'

If she is hoping for Zahid to say he will rescue Tanveer, she doesn't hear it. Even Amaan, who cares for her as a sister, hasn't offered. It is truly up to her. She is the only one who can save Tanveer.

Chapter 26

After a rest at Nana-ji's house, Shahana picks up her belongings and takes Zahid to Mr Pervaiz. She knows Aunty Rabia will not let him sleep in her house and he can't stay alone when he is so weak. He has managed to walk down the mountain but could he hunt? Mr Pervaiz lives alone; his daughters are married and living with their husbands' families. If he is surprised that she should bring a refugee for him to look after, he doesn't show it.

'A jao, come,' he says to them both, but Shahana doesn't go inside.

When she returns to Aunty Rabia's house, Ayesha is working on the computer. 'Come and see,' she says, and shows Shahana the screen. Shahana reads the words she wrote on the piece of paper, typed up on the website as a story. 'My Brother Tanveer,' she reads at the top. 'I have the responsibility for my nine-year-old brother, Tanveer. He has weak lungs, and I embroider shawls for a cloth merchant to make money to buy his food and medicine. Now Tanveer is lost and I believe the cloth merchant has him working on a carpet loom. I do not have enough money to buy him out of bondage. But I will die if I do not get my brother back. I cannot live like this where there is no peace or justice and little boys are abducted. My brother is my only relative. We are orphans of the conflict.'

There is silence while Shahana thinks. Underneath the story is her first name, with the words 'age fourteen, Neelum Valley' beside it. It is the first time she realises she is fourteen. She hasn't noticed that they have passed the part of winter when the forest burnt at her birth.

'Will I get into trouble?' she asks.

Ayesha smiles. 'No, this is a safe website for people who care about us. Look' – she clicks on an arrow – 'here is my story.'

Shahana reads that too. It is about Ayesha's father and the agony she feels over missing him, not knowing if he is alive or dead, and the prejudice she and her mother have had to endure.

'Thank you, it does feel good to tell the story,' Shahana says, even though her heart is beating too fast.

'Ji, and it may help someone else not to feel so alone.'

At that the tears dribble down Shahana's face and she sniffs.

'Shahana?'

'It is just that I did feel alone.' She gives Ayesha a watery smile.

Ayesha slips her arm around Shahana's back. 'You may have felt alone but you have done so much – you have climbed a barrier to reach me and to share your story with the world. Maybe someone who sees it will be able to help.'

Shahana doesn't think that will happen. Even the people she knows can't help. Who else will give a thought to the plight of children at the top of the world in a mountain valley, especially in the middle of winter? Her heart jolts. She hasn't time to wait for someone to see the story on the website. Mr Nadir will probably move Tanveer to a proper factory. She hopes Ayesha will understand what she is about to do. While Ayesha works on the computer, Shahana sits on the bed and takes out the dupatta and spool of gold thread. She threads the needle and embroiders around the remaining side.

—o—o—o—

In the morning Shahana goes out with a bucket to milk Rani and say goodbye. Rani gently butts her head against her arm. Shahana rests her forehead against Rani's flank as she used to. 'Rani, if only things were different, if Ummie and Irfan, Abu and Nana-ji hadn't died.'

Later, she goes to see Zahid. She stands at the door, fiddling with her hands. Mr Pervaiz draws her inside and greets her. 'Wa alaikum assalam,' she murmurs in response.

Zahid is sitting on the floor eating from a tray filled with small dishes of food. It is how her mother often served their khana.

'Baitho, sit,' Mr Pervaiz says. 'Eat with us.' There is

rice, dhal, chicken and yoghurt. Shahana dips a piece of bread into the chicken curry and pops it into her mouth. She hasn't had chicken since the last Eid when Nana-ji was alive.

'Are you okay?' Zahid says when she finishes her mouthful. It is hard for her to think this is the last time she will see him. She will send Tanveer to Aunty Rabia's and then she will be able to face anything knowing she has done her best for Tanveer.

She gives Zahid a nod. 'Are you feeling better?' she asks.

'Ji.' He is telling the truth. She can see he is rested and looks as if he is ready to run outside and hunt. She stops a sigh just in time.

Mr Pervaiz frowns at the brown paper bag by her side. 'Where are you going, beti?'

It is the first time he has called her daughter. Her heart grows still as she stares at him. If only he were her father and she could tell him everything and let him handle Mr Nadir. But she is realising there are not many men who will confront Mr Nadir like her father did.

'My hands are better and I need to get more embroidery work from Mr Nadir.' She bites her lip. Why did she say that? Zahid has narrowed his eyes and Mr Pervaiz looks uncertain.

'Be careful, beti,' he says. 'Mr Nadir is not a man to be trifled with. He has powerful business partners and can bring anyone down with an order. I would rather you didn't go there.'

Mr Pervaiz is not her father and can't forbid her to

do anything but Shahana nods respectfully. When she finishes eating, she stands. 'Shukriya,' she says before she gives Zahid one last glance.

∘–∘–∘

Shahana opens the door to Mr Nadir's shop. He isn't there but she walks in anyway. Without his presence in the room she sees things not easily noticed when he fills the room: the jewellery in the glass case under the counter and more carpets than she remembered rolled up along the back wall. She hears voices coming from the adjoining room, then Mr Nadir enters the shop.

'Ah, Shahana, daughter of Anwar Khalif.'

Shahana glances at him warily. Her father's name helps her to stand taller, but why does Mr Nadir seem amused?

'I can guess why you have come at last,' he says.

'M–my hands are getting better,' Shahana says. She puts the paper bag on the counter. 'I've brought back the dupatta.'

Mr Nadir's smirk fades slightly. He takes the dupatta out of the bag and scrutinises it. His eyebrows rise. 'Even with injured hands, your stitches are almost as good.' He puts the scarf down and regards her. 'So, what else do you have to say?'

Shahana licks her bottom lip. Is she brave enough to follow her plan?

'I would like the money for the work on the dupatta.'

Without shifting his gaze from her, he takes a note from his pocket.

166

Shahana doesn't take it. 'Ten rupees is not enough for gold work, janab.'

His eyes bore into her but she does not flinch. Amaan's piercing stares have taught her to stand firm.

Mr Nadir pulls out another ten rupee note. Shahana suspects there should be three, but his face is growing darker, so she takes it.

'Shukriya. Now—' She swallows.

'Now what?' Mr Nadir cuts in, impatience bringing his brows lower.

She takes a deep breath. 'I want to see my brother go out that door before I accept the marriage proposal.' She gestures to the outside door. She has to make sure Tanveer is there before she bargains.

Mr Nadir's mouth drops open, then he laughs. It isn't a laugh Shahana wants to join in with. 'Who are you to ask for terms? I can keep both of you. Why should I let the boy go?'

'With respect, janab, I will not accept otherwise, and you can make more money from my marriage than in all the years you will have my brother.' She could see the calculations whizzing behind his eyes. Would he believe her? 'And besides,' she adds, 'Mrs Sheikh will never do business with you again if you do not.' Shahana thinks Aunty Rabia and Ayesha won't do business with him anyway, once they find out he has her.

Mr Nadir's silence is nerve-racking. Has he taken the bait? Or, like a fox, will he outwit her?

Mr Nadir's dark look clears but this brings no comfort to Shahana. 'Very well. I will still have my revenge on your father for setting up business against me. I will take his precious daughter instead.' He strides to the door of the adjoining room and barks an order.

In a few minutes Tanveer appears in the doorway.

'Oh.' It takes Shahana a moment to react. Then she rushes to him. 'Are you okay?' He looks pale, as though he has been in a cave for a week.

He nods with a wary eye on Mr Nadir. 'Can I come home now? I don't like it here.' He whispers, but still Shahana can hear his raspy breathing. She pokes the twenty rupees into his qameez pocket.

'You must run to Aunty Rabia's,' she whispers back. 'Straight away. I will come later.'

She stands up and faces Mr Nadir, pulling Tanveer behind her. Will he still let Tanveer go or will he change his mind before Tanveer reaches the door? Mr Nadir is watching her as if observing a strange life form.

'Your father was the same, that stupid, arrogant sense of right and honour. And I see you have it too. It will get you nowhere with your husband.' He sneers, as if he has thought of something amusing, but Shahana knows it is not for her benefit. He switches his gaze to Tanveer. 'How touching. I am sorry to lose your talent, boy, but this is not the end. You can go now but you won't be able to feed yourself. You'll be back.'

'Go,' Shahana whispers. 'Run!'

But he hangs on to her. 'You're coming too?'

'Later. I must do some business first.' She hopes he will forgive her lie.

Mr Nadir makes a move towards them and Shahana pushes Tanveer out the door. He turns just the once as he is going and she forces herself to smile at him.

—o—o—o—

'So, Shahana Anwar Khalif, do you accept the marriage proposal?'

She hesitates only slightly, then lifts her chin. 'Ji, janab.'

'Actually, there are three men who want to marry you.' He is holding his hands together as if in a silent clap.

Shahana feels her legs sag.

'Of course, only one eventually will. I shall take the highest bidder.'

He is grinning at her, but a fog descends into her mind. She can hardly stand. So Amaan was right: this won't be a real marriage. Will the man even keep her after the ceremony? Mr Nadir has outwitted her after all. She ignores the shaking in her legs and forces herself to lift her head. Tanveer is safe. She will face what is to come the way she has been taught – with a show of courage, whether she feels it or not.

Chapter 27

Mr Nadir takes Shahana into the room Tanveer emerged from. The loom sits in the far corner near a high window, with three boys even younger than Tanveer tying knots and cutting wool, their curved knives a blur. The boys don't even look up as she walks through, their hands flying like little birds. A young man with a pattern in his hand stands behind the boys, checking their work. Shahana is taken into a smaller room. There are mattresses piled along the wall, but there is no window.

'This is where the little boys sleep. You can sleep here too,' Mr Nadir says. 'It will only be for a few days while I organise the marriage.' His hesitation and grin when he says 'marriage' aren't lost on Shahana.

There is a bucket of water and another bucket with a lota, a plastic jug, beside it to wash with. She doesn't dare go outside to relieve herself during the first day for she will have to pass the young man supervising the boys. Instead, she uses the bucket in the room, and empties it after the man has gone home.

That evening after the boys eat their vegetable curry and roti, they are so tired they fall onto the mattresses Shahana has put out for them. Fortunately, there is enough roti and curry for her, too.

One boy, Hanif, wakes up crying that first night. He must be only six years old. She cuddles him as if he is Tanveer. 'I wish my ummie was here,' he says between gulps.

Shahana doesn't like to ask about her in case she is dead, so she just rocks him. 'Is your father at home?' she asks instead.

The boy nods into her shawl. 'Abu was injured in the fighting. He lost his job and doesn't have the money to look after me.'

Shahana can imagine how it happened. Maybe the man secured a loan from Mr Nadir and then couldn't repay it. No doubt he was forced to give up his son, just as she has given up her freedom.

The boy speaks again. 'When Abu finds a job again he will take me home.'

Shahana doesn't say anything. Who has ever earned enough money to buy a child out of bonded labour? Hanif will have to wait until he has worked enough to pay for it himself. That could take twenty years.

Shahana counts the hours and the days. She has an embroidery square in her pocket, a needle and some thread, but she soon finishes it. She sweeps the room, but mostly she sits on top of the mattresses, wondering what Tanveer and Zahid are doing. She feels a pang when she thinks of Ayesha. She will be wondering where she is.

On the third afternoon Mr Nadir brings in clothes for her. 'Wash and put these on tonight.' There is a long embroidered skirt with a kurta, a long shirt to match. They are red and gold – a bride's clothes. They sparkle even in the low light of the room. 'I am sorry there is no wedding week for you.' He doesn't look sorry at all. Shahana knows he is only thinking of the money he will get. 'See what you can do with this.' He gives her soap, shampoo and a hairbrush, make-up, and clips for her hair – all things from his shop. 'I suppose you've never used make-up before.' He says this while hanging a mirror on the wall.

It is true Shahana has never worn make-up, but her mother did. If she was still alive, she'd be showing Shahana how to do all those things women do and this marriage wouldn't be happening at all. Only the thought of Tanveer being safe brings her some peace of mind. As Mr Nadir leaves her to wash and dress she tries to close her mind against thoughts of what might have been. This is the path she has been forced to take and she will have to learn to live with it.

When Shahana is finished and has tucked the piece of embroidery into her waistband as a keepsake, she looks into the mirror. She sees a girl's face framed by a gold dupatta, cheaper than the one she embroidered, with red lips and white skin with kohl surrounding her eyes. She imagined her face as a piece of embroidery and has applied the make-up as carefully as she sews.

The girl in the mirror looks sad, but that is the way a bride should look, as she has to leave her home. Shahana hopes the man who bids the highest is kind, but the richest men are rarely the kindest.

This is not what her parents planned for her. She would have had a wedding with families involved, a mehndi night when female relatives and friends would have come to bath her, apply henna patterns to her hands and feet and sing wedding songs; the groom arriving next day on a white horse with the wedding band of horns and drums. In her wildest dreams the groom would be Zahid, but she knows that dreams don't come true. Only nightmares do.

The boys come in tired and hungry. 'You look like a bride,' Hanif says. 'Are you going away?'

He cries and Shahana hugs him. 'I'm sorry,' she says. 'Brides always go away.'

The food comes and the boys eat, even Hanif, but Shahana can't swallow a bite.

Mr Nadir finally returns. 'Accha, you have done a good job as usual. Maybe making yourself beautiful will be useful in the future.' He isn't sneering this time, and she glances up in surprise. 'If times were different—' But he doesn't say what would happen if times were different, and Shahana is sure she doesn't want to know. She follows him into the shop. The electric lights are off; gas lamps shine a warm glow over the room.

In the centre of the room is a carpet and a few metres from the carpet are three chairs. Three men are sitting in the chairs. They look like the men with shiny haircuts, dressed in long achkan coats, that Shahana has seen on TV. One man is smoking.

'Stand in the middle of the carpet, Shahana,' Mr Nadir says.

'This is Shahana,' Mr Nadir says to the men. 'She is an innocent orphan who has been living in the forest.' It is the kindest she has heard him speak, but she knows it is just to get the highest price. Mr Nadir asks her to walk slowly in front of each man. One cups her chin and turns her face sideways; another asks her to turn a full circle. At least she is not asked to smile – she couldn't have managed that. Then she returns to the carpet. She doesn't know how long the ceremony will take and hopes it isn't too long – she is afraid her legs will fold up. They haven't been the same since the avalanche.

'Can she dance?' the third man asks.

'She is very talented,' Mr Nadir says, 'she will easily learn.'

The second man smiles at her. Shahana thinks it is worse than Mr Nadir's smile.

One man says fifty thousand rupees; the next says one hundred thousand. It sounds like a fortune to Shahana. Money like that could build a proper school. There is a silence and Mr Nadir shakes his head sadly. 'She is worth much more than this, my friends. Where would you get such a precious jewel, so untouched by the world? Just imagine—'

Mr Nadir doesn't get to say what the men should imagine as the door of his shop is pushed open. *Not*

174

another man? Shahana thinks. Then she sees who it is. She presses her lips tightly together so no sound will slip out. It is Amaan.

'What do you think you are doing?' Mr Nadir says. His voice is tight with fury. 'This is a private function. Chello, leave this instant.'

Amaan strolls into the room and looks around. He has his Kalashnikov over his right shoulder, but his right arm cradles it so his hand rests on the trigger. 'No wonder you have such precious carpets if this is what you do in your spare time.' He takes a chair from the corner with one hand and brings it to face Shahana. 'Is this not an illegal practice? You wouldn't be taking advantage of this child because she's an orphan?'

'Get out!' Mr Nadir's face is turning purple.

'Not until I take this child with me.' He emphasises the word 'child' and one of the men swiftly stands behind his chair, a wary eye on Amaan's Kalashnikov.

'You wouldn't have the money,' Mr Nadir says, rage making his voice tight. 'I know what you are – you are just a jihadi, causing trouble. You lot think you can put your nose into our affairs. Well, you're not one of us. You have no right to ruin my business.'

Amaan stands and the Kalashnikov falls easily into his hands. His voice rises over Mr Nadir's. 'Children have the right to be safe and everyone has a duty to protect them. And I think the police outside will agree with me.'

At that the suited men all slip out the door.

'If I hear you have interfered with this child again I

shall kill you.' Amaan says this so simply that even Mr Nadir must know he tells the truth.

Yet Mr Nadir splutters. 'You won't get away with this – I can have you killed. You've crossed the wrong man.'

'You can tell that to the police.' He gestures to Shahana to come to him.

She glances at Mr Nadir. Can he stop her? But he is standing as if his legs are made of ice. She walks to Amaan as quickly as she can without tripping over the long skirt. The door bursts open and two policemen stride in. One looks at Amaan as if he'd like to arrest him, but Amaan says, 'This is my sister.' He points to Mr Nadir. 'There is your criminal who tried to sell her.'

'Mr Nadir Khan?' asks the other police officer as Shahana slips out the door after Amaan. She doesn't hear any more.

Amaan takes his huge shawl from his shoulder and wraps it around her, then picks up a backpack and guides her to the road.

'I thought I told you not to go near him,' he says.

'I didn't think you'd be able to do anything.'

He makes a sound like a sigh. 'It was a brave thing you did, but foolish. You could have been in a big city in a week.'

'But I had to get Tanveer out. Mr Nadir was going to move him to a factory. I would never have found him.'

'I should have blown up his blasted shop. He deserves it.'

'I'm glad you didn't. There are three more boys living there, even younger than Tanveer.'

'I am joking only. I am finished with that life.'

There is a silence while Shahana wonders about the police. She doesn't remember when she last saw them in the village. 'Where do the police come from?'

'I don't know. I saw their jeep heading for the bazaar before I entered the shop. I was bluffing about them being outside.'

'Mr Nadir will try to bribe them.'

They walk past Mr Pervaiz's house and Shahana wonders what Zahid is doing.

'How did you know I was there?' she asks.

'I imagine you will hear all about it soon. You did look beautiful standing there – you would have fetched a high price.' He stops to face her, even though Shahana can't see him very well. 'I am proud to call you sister.'

When they reach Aunty Rabia's house Amaan stands with his foot on the bottom step, looking up at her. 'You must still be careful. I think the man will not bother you now that the police are involved, but I have caused him too much embarrassment and shame. I will return now across the mountains to the Khagan Valley to look after my own sister.'

'Is that your home?'

'Close to there. You only have to look at the mountains and know that I am on the other side.' He glances away. 'All we are doing is destroying lives and a culture. This war cannot be won but no one will understand why I have given up the struggle.'

'I do,' she whispers.

'And now I owe an obligation to every orphan.' He

looks at her again. 'But I will never forget you. You are so surprising, like the snow, so pure and quiet, yet you burn with fire.'

She wants to say she won't forget him either. Instead, she takes the embroidery square out of her waistband and hands it to him. This time it is a true gift, and he tucks it in the top pocket of his qameez. He puts his hand over his heart and inclines his head, then backs a few steps before he turns away.

It is not until she can't see his shadow anymore that she opens the door.

Chapter 28

Ayesha is right by the door when Shahana pushes it open. 'Shahana, it is you. I thought I heard a noise outside.' She looks out the door. 'What happened? Tanveer said you were coming, but that was days ago.'

'Mr Nadir kept me, but I escaped.' She doesn't mention Amaan; he will be too hard to explain.

Ayesha takes her hand and leads her inside. 'These clothes – they are fit for a wedding. Was he going to marry you off after all?'

And suddenly, at the sound of Ayesha's voice, the relief of being in her house is too much. Shahana can't stop her tears. 'There were three men – they were bidding for me.'

Ayesha is almost speechless. 'How – how did you escape?'

Shahana stops and gulps. She can't name Amaan. Then she remembers the police.

'The police arrived.'

'Police?' Ayesha says the word as if it is foreign.

Shahana nods. 'They must have come from Athmuqam.'

Ayesha is quiet a moment, as if wondering how such a thing could happen. Shahana too is confused. The police rarely visit their little village.

Ayesha puts her arms around her. 'I'm so glad you are safe.'

Shahana lets the sobs takes over. What horror it was. She hadn't realised what she was walking into. After a while her crying eases. Ayesha hands her a tissue.

'Come,' Ayesha says gently. 'We must get you out of those clothes.'

'Where is Tanveer?' Shahana asks.

Ayesha gestures towards a new bed in the room. 'Asleep. It's quite late.'

Tanveer is curled up like a baby under the quilt. Shahana bends to kiss him on the forehead. 'Where did you get this bed?' she asks.

'Mr Pervaiz gave us one of his daughter's beds – they rarely visit here now. Mine is in the other room.'

Ayesha takes her hand again. 'When you've changed, there's something I want to show you. It will dry all your tears.' She can't keep the excitement from her eyes and Shahana wonders what can't wait until morning.

Soon, after dressing in one of Ayesha's outfits and washing off the make-up with special remover, Shahana sits in front of the computer.

'I know it's late but Ummie's asleep and you have to see this.' Ayesha presses some keys on the computer and the website where their stories are flickers onto the screen.

'There are more stories?' Shahana asks.

'Better than that,' Ayesha says, scrolling down with the mouse. 'Look, there's a place to put comments, and see? There are hundreds of them, all saying how sad they are, how bad our situation is. Other people have told about their own situation, too. And one of them has written an email and it has already travelled around the world to countries like Britain, Australia, Canada and even America. People are signing a petition for the government to help us.'

Shahana turns a stricken face to Ayesha. 'We will get into trouble. We will be punished.'

'No, we won't.'

'But everyone will know what is happening, what it is like here. The government will be embarrassed. Mr Nadir—'

'The government official is coming up to Athmuqam sooner than the end of winter. Look.' She shows Shahana a news item on the website. 'He is going to give us money to start a school here. Ummie will teach again.'

'What if they send Tanveer and me to an orphanage? That is why I have never told anyone how hard it is to live and to look after him.'

'Shahana, people need to know what happens to kids like us. When others know, it is harder for evil people to get away with the things they do.'

'Did someone from the website contact the police?' Shahana asks.

'I don't think so,' Ayesha murmurs. 'But this is

wonderful support. And Ummie has something to tell you tomorrow, too.'

Suddenly there is an explosion. Shahana grabs the bed as she feels the floor shudder. There's a thump, then the shelling and gunfire starts. It sounds just like the day Irfan and her mother died. 'RPGs.' She clutches Ayesha.

'It doesn't sound close,' Ayesha says, but Shahana can tell she is worried. One could get used to gunfire, but not RPGs. 'I think it is high up the mountain.'

The door opens and Shahana jumps. 'Tanveer.'

He runs to her. 'Shahji, I heard rockets.' He climbs onto her lap. 'You took so long to come home, I thought Mr Nadir had you working on the loom instead.'

'It was a little like that but I got away.' She looks up at another *whomp*, louder and closer. It sounds as if the whole mountain is falling down.

They wait, but the fighting seems to be staying on the mountain. Shahana hugs Tanveer to her, then carries him to the new bed and slips in beside him.

–o–o–o–

Shahana wakes tired in the morning, having dreamed she was holding an AK-47 Kalashnikov, about to shoot a man to save Tanveer. But the gun was too heavy and she couldn't aim it straight. Would she shoot Tanveer by accident? Half the night she couldn't tell if the sound of gunfire was in her dreams or really happening.

'Is the village safe?' she asks quietly as Ayesha comes into the room to look out of the window. Aunty Rabia and Tanveer are still sleeping.

'There's fog, but nothing seems different.'

Later, as they eat breakfast on cushions in the main room, Tanveer chatters. Shahana is realising that this is his way of shutting out things he is frightened of. 'Tanveer,' she says, 'the fighting didn't reach the village. We are safe.'

He nods and bites into his roti.

'I am so glad you are home with us,' Aunty Rabia says.

Shahana smiles at her as she lifts her teacup. Aunty Rabia is like her old self.

'Ayesha and I have something to tell you both.'

They are smiling so Shahana can tell it is good news. She wonders if it is about Ayesha's father.

'We want you to always live with us and be Ayesha's sister and brother.' Aunty Rabia watches them expectantly. Shahana tries to put the cup on the tray but it clatters and spills. She wants to show how happy she is but tears come instead. Tanveer jumps up and hugs Aunty Rabia.

'Thank you, Aunty-ji,' Shahana says through her tears. 'We shall always try to bring you honour and happiness.'

Ayesha hugs them both. 'I love you like a sister already.'

—o—o—o—

Shahana decides to take Tanveer to see Mr Pervaiz. She is hoping to see Zahid too, and she has warned Tanveer that Zahid will need to go home. She expects he will act

183

as he did when Nana-ji was ill, insisting that Zahid won't leave, but he keeps silent, as if he doesn't hear her.

Ayesha stops them at the door. 'I should come too. That way if Mr Nadir should try to grab you, he will think twice, knowing there will be a witness.'

'We will not go through the bazaar – we'll take a shortcut. Then you won't have to worry.'

Shahana and Tanveer creep behind the houses, climb across stone fences and walk in thick snow until they reach the back of Mr Pervaiz's house. Their shoes and legs are wet, but they are safe.

Mr Pervaiz's eyes widen when he sees Shahana. 'Zahid,' he calls. 'Come, Shahana is free.' He ushers them inside and fills his samovar to make chai. Zahid is there, watching her walk in. She feels the warmth, just like in Aunty Rabia's house. Mr Pervaiz has a gas bottle with a heater warming the room.

'Did you hear the fighting last night on the mountain?' Shahana asks.

'Ji.' Both Zahid and Mr Pervaiz nod, but Zahid frowns as well.

'What is it?' she asks.

'It was the militants' camp,' Zahid says, checking her face with a careful look.

'Good,' Mr Pervaiz says, pouring chai. 'We don't want them here causing trouble.'

'What happened? Were they attacked?' Shahana sinks onto a cushion.

'Some men bombed it, then there was fighting and of course the army had to come to finish it.' Mr Pervaiz sighs. 'There is always trouble where there are militants.'

Mr Nadir. Just as Shahana thinks it her gaze meets Zahid's and she realises that, like her, he is worried for Amaan. She leans closer to him. 'Amaan came to rescue me but I don't know how he knew I was in the shop.' She whispers it and hopes Mr Pervaiz doesn't hear her over at the stove.

'Tanveer came here before he went to Mrs Sheikh's and told me where you were.'

'Was it you who told Amaan?'

'Ji, you said he could be trusted and I hoped you were right. There was nothing else to do. But now...' He leaves the words unsaid but Shahana knows what they are. Because of her, Amaan's life is in danger. 'Mr Pervaiz couldn't go to the cloth shop. I think Mr Nadir has some power over him, but he heard what was going to happen to you and he hired a jeep to Athmuqam.'

'For the police.' Shahana stops whispering and turns to where Mr Pervaiz is putting noon chai on a tray for them. 'Mr Pervaiz, it was you who fetched the police, wasn't it? You saved me.'

He won't look at her. He takes some biscuits from a packet. 'It was a little thing only,' he says. But it isn't a little thing at all. If Mr Nadir knew he was involved, Mr Pervaiz or his business could be affected. Amaan would have had a difficult time freeing her if there were no police to threaten Mr Nadir with. He may have had to fire his gun, and then the villagers may have attacked him. Now it seems that Mr Nadir has rallied some men

185

to do that anyway. Shahana hopes Amaan got away and that the other militants think he is lost in the fighting, and won't hunt him down.

She looks up to see Zahid watching her.

'Shahana, Veer,' he says firmly, as if the words are difficult to think about. 'I must leave today. The army doctor told me something important.'

Shahana wonders if he means his heart.

'There are unmarked graves across the LoC. I will go there first and say a prayer for my father.'

'You won't know if he is there,' Shahana says.

'Maybe not, but I will pray the prayer. Then I will return to my mother. She probably thinks I am dead too.'

Shahana nods at him. 'That is a good thing to do.' She hopes the pride she feels for him shines from her eyes.

He draws Tanveer closer. 'I want to stay with you, Veer,' he says, 'but I am my mother's only son. You understand that, don't you?'

At first Tanveer is quiet and Shahana holds her breath. Always she has worried about this moment. Then Tanveer gives a nod. 'Aunty Rabia is adopting Shahji and me.'

Shahana is proud to hear him so brave, showing Zahid that they will be okay.

'I am glad to hear it.'

When they have drunk the chai, Zahid says, 'I am going to study – I want to change things, not sit all day smoking a hookah like my cousins.'

She nods at him, not wanting to leave. 'Me too,' she says.

'Live well, Shahana.'

'And you, Zahid.' His name slips out of her mouth like a sigh.

Their words mean little; the meaning is in their eyes. Shahana hopes hers show how much she will miss him.

Chapter 29

When Shahana and Tanveer return to Aunty Rabia's it is lunchtime, but the house is quiet. They creep into the big room in case Aunty Rabia is asleep, but she and Ayesha are sitting together on the bed. Ayesha raises her head and Shahana can see the tear tracks on her face. Shahana rushes to her. 'What is the matter?'

Ayesha opens the computer beside her and shows Shahana an official website. 'The government has posted a list of men who have died in police or army custody. It is a small list, but it is a start.'

'And?' Shahana is feeling the fear that Ayesha must have felt when she saw the list.

'Papa's name is on it.' Ayesha's voice turns into a squeak and she hides her face in Aunty Rabia's chest. Shahana puts the computer on the floor and sits beside Ayesha, slipping an arm around her. Then she has an awful thought. *Will this upset Aunty Rabia so much that she will never go outside?*

'I'm so sorry,' Shahana says. She stumbles over the

words and wonders if Zahid's father's name is on a list in Kashmir, too. Tanveer sits on the floor and lays his head in Ayesha's lap.

Ayesha sits up straighter with a hand on Tanveer's hair. 'We suspected it.'

'Yes,' Aunty Rabia says.

Shahana watches her to see if she will say more.

'Now we can have the funeral at least. The best thing would have been to have him returned to us, but this is still better than not knowing at all.'

That afternoon, just as if he had died that very day, Aunty Rabia, Ayesha, Shahana and Tanveer walk with Mr Pervaiz and the mullah to the cemetery. They have no body wrapped in the calico cloth that Mr Pervaiz carries in front of them, but in it is a photo of Ayesha's father, verses from the Quran, and letters that Ayesha and Aunty Rabia wrote to him to say how they feel.

Other people, mostly women from the village, follow them. Usually men go to funerals but there are more women than men now. If Mr Nadir is there, Shahana doesn't notice – she keeps her head covered and watches the ground, which is like ice. It is a good thing they only have a small bundle to bury. It would have taken a huge machine to dig a bigger hole.

Afterwards, while Aunty Rabia is speaking to some ladies for the first time in two years, Shahana takes Tanveer aside and shows him where their family grave-site is. Since Nana-ji died she has never visited, never wanted to be reminded of how they all died. 'This is where Ummie and Abu are,' she says. 'And Irfan.' She stops.

'And here is Nana-ji,' Tanveer says. 'I remember.'

Her eyes water as she realises it is almost a year since he died. 'It will be different now, Tanveer. We will be able to study and do all the things Ummie and Abu and Nana-ji wished for us to do.'

'Shahji, will you call me Veer now?'

He sounds older and it takes her a moment to answer. 'As you wish – Veer.'

'Can we look at Nana-ji's house again?'

'We will go tomorrow, inshallah.'

⚬—⚬—⚬

The next day, Shahana and Tanveer leave Ayesha and Aunty Rabia in the house to grieve with some village women, and walk across the log bridge. The water is iced over on the sides, with a narrow stream rushing down the middle. It wouldn't be good to fall in there today; they are approaching the last sister of winter, the coldest and deadliest of all. They climb the lower slopes of the mountain; crocus leaves are shooting up through the thinner snow and there are buds on the chinar trees. The almonds are already in pink blossom. They pass the spring and Nana-ji's rosebushes, then they stop in shock.

'Where is the house?' Tanveer cries.

They run up the logs, but that is all there is. The house has fallen in on itself. It looks like a wood pile ready for the fire. Someone has thrown a grenade in it.

'The militants. Did they do this? Or did it happen in the fighting?' Tanveer asks.

'I don't think so. It's too far away from the camp.' People will say it was the militants, of course. No one will point the finger at the person Shahana thinks has ordered this. Did he hope they'd be there and be killed? Or is it a reminder that he is still powerful and can do anything he wants?

'Come,' she says, her voice flat. 'We'll go back. There is nothing here for us now.'

'Wait.' Tanveer runs to where the other side of the house was. 'Shahji, look.'

She makes her way through the snow to see what he has found. He is crouching over the ground. 'It's the potato we planted, Zahid and me. It's grown.'

Tears flood her eyes as she sees the lone shoot. Such a tiny strip of green in a white landscape. Tanveer stands up. 'I will check if it survives and when I am grown, I will rebuild Nana-ji's house.' He stands there with his legs apart, just like the day he asked her to save Zahid. Watching him, she thinks how there are shadows, things that have to be lived with, yet there is also light.

She draws him close to her and feels the love swelling in her chest. It hurts, as if her heart isn't used to stretching so wide. 'That will be good, Veer.'

He takes her hand and they walk past the spring, down the mountain towards the log bridge.

Author's note

For ten years I worked as an aid worker in the Middle East and most of that time was spent in Khyber Pakhtunkhwa in Northern Pakistan. We lived in Abbottabad close to Azad Kashmir, but we were not allowed to cross the border. It wasn't until 2006 when I was on an Asialink Writing Fellowship, and the border opened for aid workers helping with the aftermath of the 2005 earthquake, that I was able to visit Muzaffarabad in Azad Kashmir. There was a huge amount of damage, but I could see it had once been a beautiful place. Little is written in papers about how the Kashmiri conflict affects children, but there are some reports on the Web that can be accessed. I wanted to tell these children's stories, albeit fictitiously, so other young people in peaceful countries like Australia can understand and care. And maybe, as Ayesha says, knowing these stories can help.

The war over Kashmir is the longest-running conflict in the world today, and possibly the least well known or understood. For centuries Kashmir had a culture that included many faiths. This culture is called Kashmiriyat and it managed to combine the diverse faiths in harmony and tolerance. Muslim lived next door to Hindu and they respected each other's faiths and festivals. Included were Buddhists, Hindus, Sufi, Sikhs and Muslims – it was like a brotherhood to fight the isolation of the high mountain region.

The Kashmiri conflict is a difficult one to write about as there are many different points of view. India believes all Kashmir is part of India and calls Azad Kashmir 'Pakistani-occupied Kashmir'; Pakistan believes all of Kashmir was meant to be part of Pakistan due to the 1947 Partition and calls Jammu and Kashmir 'Indian-occupied Kashmir'. The Kashmiri people themselves have differing points of view, but many would prefer to have freedom, independence and self-government without interference from either India or Pakistan. Zahid calls his homeland Kashmir, the name it was always called.

Historical details of the conflict differ according to what nationality the writer is, and accounts are often contradictory. However, it can be said that this conflict began in 1947 and has caused two major wars between India and Pakistan (1947 and 1965) and almost caused another in 1999. In 1988 Kashmiri militants committed to independence launched attacks against Indian rule. Other jihadi militants, supplied with training and arms by Pakistan, infiltrated Kashmir and joined in the fighting. Militant groups are divided between fighting for independence from India or fighting for for becoming part of Pakistan. India constructed the barrier or fence along the Line of Control (LoC) which runs along the border between Azad Kashmir and Jammu and Kashmir to stop foreign militants from infiltrating Kashmir. The barrier was finished in 2004.

The ratio of troops to civilians in Kashmir is the highest in the world, with 450000 to 750000 Indian troops employed.[1] There are many widows and half-widows (those women whose husbands are missing), and the children suffer, as *Shahana* shows. Besides the conflict there are also those who prey upon the disadvantaged, and many orphans are sold into forced labour, kidnapped or become victims of violence and abuse. Boys face recruitment and girls face early marriage. Children are disillusioned by the violence and have many health problems, including post-traumatic stress disorder. Many sources say there are over 100000 orphans in Kashmir but the UK-based NGO Save the Children recently stated that the number of orphans in Kashmir is as high as 214000.[2] Azad Kashmir has set up camps for refugees and orphans from Kashmir and Jammu, and Kashmir has many orphanages.

One fourteen-year-old Kashmiri said, 'I want the government and opposition groups to avoid destroying the lives of children by depriving them of their parents.' This boy wants to be a doctor to help other orphans.

Central Asia Insititute, a non-profit organisation, believes the way to peace and hope is through education. CAI is building schools in Azad Kashmir. Read about this in Greg Mortenson's *Stones into Schools* (Penguin 2009, and at ikat.org). UNICEF is also building schools in Azad Kashmir and opened sixteen in 2011 (*The Express Tribune*, 26 May, 2011). Check out UNICEF's work to help children in Kashmir at unicef.org.au.

1 'Responding to Gendered Violence in Kashmir' (Association of Parents of Disappeared Persons, July 2011).
2 Altaf, Sana. 'Thousands orphaned by poverty in Kashmir' (*Inter Press Service*, 9 January 2013).

Timeline

1947 Partition of Indian subcontinent: Union of India and Dominion of Pakistan.

Indo–Pakistani War of 1947 First war over Kashmir. The Maharajah of the state of Jammu and Kashmir asks India for help, relinquishing control over defence, communication and foreign affairs until a plebiscite can be held. Ceasefire line divides Kashmir.

1948 India takes dispute over Kashmir territory to the United Nations Security Council. Pakistan and India agree to withdraw troops behind ceasefire line.

1949 Ceasefire results in Indian control of most of the Kashmir valley. Pakistan controls Azad Kashmir and northern territories.

1957 India declares the State of Jammu and Kashmir an integral part of India.

Indo–Pakistani War of 1965 Kashmiris stage anti-India riots. Pakistan launches 'Operation Grand Slam' to capture India-controlled Kashmir. Violence erupts in Kashmir Valley.

1966 Kashmiri nationalists form Jammu and Kashmir National Liberation Front (NLF).

1972 Simla Agreement: Line of Control (LoC) is the redesignated ceasefire line. Fighting continues – LoC now one of the most violent and dangerous borderlines in the world.

1987–1990 Kashmir Insurgency: Revolts by young Kashmiris recruited by renamed Jammu and Kashmir National Liberation Front (JKNLF).

1990s Estimated 500 000 Indian security forces deployed in the Kashmir Valley, increased violence by both sides, tens of thousands of civilian casualties. Almost a million Kashmiris protest against Indian occupation. Construction of the 740 km Indian LoC separation barrier begins, and is finished in 2004.

1998 Both India and Pakistan conduct nuclear tests.

1999 Kargil War: Armed conflict between India and Pakistan along the LoC results in more than one thousand casualties. Pakistan withdraws under international pressure.

2000 Unilateral ceasefire declared in Jammu and Kashmir. Peace talks begin in Srinagar to end the five decades of hostilities but are short-lived as fighting begins after two weeks.

2001 Two Pakistani militant groups blamed for a deadly attack on the Indian Parliament. India calls upon Pakistan to close its terrorist training camps. Troops mass at the LoC and the worst fighting occurs as India shells Pakistani military positions.

2003 India and Pakistan agree to a ceasefire across the LoC.

2005 Pakistan earthquake – epicentre near Muzaffarabad, Azad Kashmir: 79 000 dead, 106 000 injured, 6000 schools destroyed.

2006 Second round of Indo–Pakistani peace talks.

2007 Amnesty International reports gross
human rights violations by both sides.

2010 Kashmir unrest: protests in Kashmir
Valley in Indian-administered Kashmir
result in 112 deaths. Killing of young
Kashmiri student Tufail Ahmad Mattoo
spikes further protests, with more than 270
Indian security officers attacked by stone-
throwing mobs of youths.

An amnesty for fighters from Indian-
administered Kashmir is announced,
allowing many to return home.

2012 Tourists begin to return to Kashmir
despite continued ceasefire violations at the
India–Pakistan border.

Glossary

abu; abu-ji dad, father; dear or respected father

accha good

achkan knee-length jacket or coat

a jao come

Angrezi English

Alhamdulillah praise be to God

aloo potato

assalamu alaikum peace be upon you

azadi freedom

azan call to prayer

baitho sit

beti daughter

bijily electricity

bismillah in the name of God

chai; noon chai spiced tea; salt tea

charpoy a string bed

chello go

chitta leopard

chup quiet

dekshi cooking pot

dhal lentil curry

dupatta a long silk scarf

Eid ul Fitr a religious holiday to mark the end
of Ramadan

haram forbidden

inshallah if God wills

Jahanam hell

jaldi quickly

janab sir

jawan a teenage boy

ji; ji hahn yes

ji nahin no

jinn a spirit which can be good or evil, and take human or animal form

kangri fire pot

khana food

kharmosh quiet

Khuda hafiz goodbye, may God be your protector

koi hai? is anyone there?

kurta a long shirt

lota jug

mehndi henna

mullah Muslim religious leader or priest

nahin no

namdah felt rug

nana; nana-ji mother's father; dear or respected mother's father

nay no

pheran woollen winter robe

qameez long shirt or tunic

roti bread

saag spinach

samovar copper kettle with burning coals in a central cylinder to heat water or chai

shalwar loose trousers

shukriya   thank you

shikara   wooden oar-driven boat

teik hai   okay; fine

ummie; ummie-ji   mum, mother; dear or respected mother

wa alaikum assalam   and upon you be peace

zarur   certainly

Find out more about...

Children in Kashmir

'Kashmiri Children Appeal to India and Pakistan to Maintain Peace Agreement on LoC', *Eurasia Review*, 22 September, 2012

Mitchell, Jane. *Chalkline*, Walker Books, London, 2009

Mortenson, Greg & David Oliver Relin. *Three Cups of Tea*, Penguin Young Reader's Group, New York, 2009

http://www.unicef.org/pakistan

http://www.youtube.com/watch?v=A4TyoEP8Nlo

Child labour

D'Adamo, Francesco. *Iqbal*, Atheneum Books for Young Readers: Simon & Schuster, New York, 2001

Hawke, Rosanne. *Mountain Wolf*, HarperCollins, Sydney, 2012

http://www.unicef.org.au/About-Us/What-We-Do/Protection.aspx

Forced marriage

Ali, Nujood & Delphine Minoui. *I am Nujood, Age 10 and Divorced*, Random House, NSW, 2010

Hawke, Rosanne. *Marrying Ameera*, HarperCollins, Sydney, 2010

Whelan, Gloria. *Homeless Bird*, HarperCollins, New York, 2000

Line of Control

news.bbc.co.uk/2/hi/south_asia/377916.stm
insightonconflict.org/conflicts/kashmir

Acknowledgements

A big thank you to Lyn White and Jacinta di Mase for thinking of me to write for the Through My Eyes series. Thanks also to Eva Mills and the wonderful team at Allen & Unwin.

Thank you, Frank Lyman, for your ever-helpful military advice.

In researching for *Shahana*, I am indebted to Rumer Godden's 'A Winter Diary' published for the first time with a 2002 reprinting of her 1953 novel *Kingfishers Catch Fire* (London: Pan Macmillan).

I was also inspired by John Isaac's beautiful photographs in *Vale of Kashmir* (New York: WW Norton, 2008).

Dr Martin Luther King's first quote at the beginning comes from Stephen B. Oates, *Let the Trumpet Sound: a life of Martin Luther King* (New York: Harper & Row, 1982). His second quote is from an address delivered in Alabama, 1957.

The line 'When you have faced the impossible only the possible remains', which inspired Nana-ji's words, is from Sudha Koul, *The Tiger Ladies* (Boston: Headline, 2002, p. 30).

The song Shahana sings is inspired by Emperor Jahangir's 1620 poem about Kashmir, 'The garden nymphs were brilliant', which can be found online in *The Memoirs of Jahangir* volume 2, translated by Alexander Rogers and edited by Henry Beveridge, 1909.

The words Ayesha sings are from the song, 'Mere Haath Mein' (In My Hand) from the movie *Fanaa* by Kunal Kohli (Mumbai: Yash Raj Films, 2006).

The story that Shahana tells is based on 'The Tale of a King' in the 1923 volume of *Hatim's Tales: Kashmiri Stories and Songs* by Sir Aurel Stein (New Delhi: Gyan Books, 1989).

The story of the haunted mosque can be found in *Tales of Kashmir* by Rev J. Hinton Knowles (London: Trubner, 1889).

The story of the stone princess is inspired by an anecdotal story of the same name from the area of Kotli, Azad Kashmir, and also by the legendary Princess Sharda after whom Mount Sharda in the Neelum Valley was named. There is also a story called 'Four Princes Turned into Stone' in Knowles's *Tales of Kashmir*.

Tanveer's stories are his own.

Islamic spelling is according to the *Islamic Dictionary* (islamic-dictionary.com).

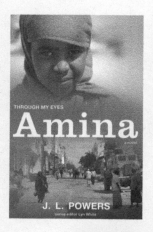

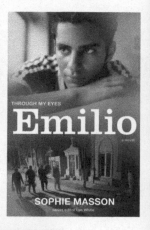
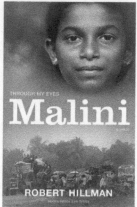
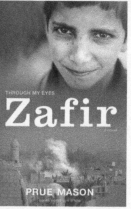